I0649008

COMING TO TERMS

Coming to Terms

A collection of short stories
by

TOM GLENN

Adelaide Books
New York / Lisbon
2020

COMING TO TERMS
A collection of short stories
By Tom Glenn

Copyright © by Tom Glenn
Cover design © 2020 Adelaide Books

Published by Adelaide Books, New York / Lisbon
adelaidebooks.org

Editor-in-Chief
Stevan V. Nikolic

All rights reserved. No part of this book may be reproduced in any manner whatsoever without written permission from the author except in the case of brief quotations embodied in critical articles and reviews.

For any information, please address Adelaide Books
at info@adelaidebooks.org
or write to:
Adelaide Books
244 Fifth Ave. Suite D27
New York, NY, 10001

ISBN: 978-1-952570-94-0

Printed in the United States of America

Contents

Foreword

Coming to Terms tells the stories of men and women confronted with pain as a consequence of love and hate, goodness and evil. Each finds a way to go on living, however imperfectly. None is left unscathed.

All these tales come from my life, as a husband, father, soldier, and caregiver to the dying. Each major character is drawn from people I've known. My hope is that you and I, both, can learn from the choices these people made.

The Gift of the Father

Mike Loring cleared his throat. "John Loring, please."

The nurse behind the counter went on reading, her painted eyes straight out of a nineteen-sixties Maybelline ad. "Visiting hours—" She glanced up. "Sorry, Reverend." She squinted at the inside wall of the counter. "606. Halfway down the corridor."

Past the philodendron, caladium, and rubber plants down the creaking linoleum to Room 606. Mike pushed the door open. Inside, the orange blossom air freshener was tinged with sweat, iodine, and a stench he couldn't identify. The walls and sheets were dead white, the blankets and chair the color of undiluted bleach. T-shaped frames, one on each side of the bed, dangled plastic bags and tubes, all feeding into the creature below them. A high-pitched whine punctuated by contorted breathing came from the cranked-up bed. Beneath the softly throbbing tubes, an old man lay on his side, his eyes closed. His hair, what there was of it, his eyebrows and eyelashes were as white as the wall, his yellow skin translucent as candle wax, his body small, like a stunted and withered child who had bypassed maturity and moved directly to old age.

Mike stood beside the bed and spoke his father's name. "John Loring."

The whine ceased. The plastic bags rustled. The old man quivered, and his eyes opened. The outer edges of the irises were olive green. Nearer the pupils the color faded to white, but the pupils themselves were black slits. Eyes Mike hadn't seen for almost thirty years.

The yellow hand squeezed the call button pinned to the pillow. "No visitors," the old man said in a papery voice. "I told them."

"Yes?" said the speaker above the bed.

"My shot."

"Not yet, Mr. Loring."

The eyes closed. The jaw tightened. The hands moved among the tubes, too feeble to attack them. "Somebody's bothering me." The old man fixed Mike in a sidelong glare. "A priest."

Mike grasped the bed's chrome railing. "I came because—"

"Get the fuck out." The quivering yellow fingers pumped the call button over and over.

"Papa!"

The old man's hands stopped grabbling. His eyes read Mike's face and moved to the Roman collar, then snapped shut. "How'd you find me?"

"The guy who admitted you listed Mom as next of kin."

The nurse with the Maybelline eyes appeared in her silent white shoes. "Mr. Loring, why don't you let the reverend talk to you? Then we'll have our shot." She took the old man's hand and bent toward him. "You want some nice, cold apple juice?"

"I want my shot," John said.

The nurse gave Mike a knowing smile. "Can I get you anything, Reverend?"

"No, thanks."

She padded away, leaving behind the scent of Tabu.

Mike sat in the chair next to the bed, put his elbows on his knees, smiled tentatively. The old man lay tense, eyes still slammed shut.

Mike cleared his throat. "When Mom told me, I was afraid I might be too late. I tried to get her to come, Papa."

"Don't call me that."

The taut body was motionless.

Mike scanned the room. No sign of hope. A book on the bed stand. Mike turned it over. *Historie of England.* Inside he found a tattered snapshot of himself as a toddler. He rested his fingertips on John's arm. "Papa, talk to me."

John put his hand to his forehead. The fingers, fixed, already dead, scraped the skin. "You want my help while there's still time. A last blessing, forgiveness . . ." John aped a sardonic smile. "Closure. *Libera me, Domine.* 'Who will rid me of this troublesome priest?'"

Mike caught his breath. "You remember. 'And the knights there assembled . . .' *Historie of England.* Henry II."

"I remember nothing. I want you out of here. Another parasite, more toxoplasma eating my brain."

"'And the knights there assembled withdrew, saying to one another, "We know the king's will."' Papa, say it. 'And when the king . . .'"

John's lips pulled back from his teeth. "Worse than nagging. Slobbering, fawning, cringing. I want to die without being badgered. I have no son. I am no father. I'm a queer, a homo, a fucking fairy. I don't want you. *Just leave me alone!*"

Mike bowed his head and put his hand over his father's. "Please."

John yanked his hand away. The plastic bags swung wild. The old man stretched his jaws and howled. Mike leaped to his feet. The nurse and a man in white bolted though the door.

Mike stumbled out of the room. He clattered down the hall and past the nurses' station, sideswiping the potted plants. A woman in sickly green scrubs and surgical cap got off the elevator and scanned him with unsmiling eyes. He slipped past her onto the elevator. At the ground level, he finally found the glass doors to the street. He dashed the block to the subway, down the stairway stinking of urine, out onto the platform with the crowd spreading like a wave on the sand. A train pulled in. Just before the doors slammed, he jostled his way into a car and dropped into the first empty seat.

When his breathing slowed and the tremors eased, he found a handkerchief in his pocket and wiped the skim of sweat from his hands and forehead. A quick glance around the car told him no one was watching. He filled his lungs slowly and closed his eyes. That howl—a cry of implacable pain. It reverberated in Mike, echoed his own cries. He shook his head. *Fool.* He should have hung in there. He wouldn't let his father abandon him again.

The following night, his father's room was dark. The stench was stronger. So was the Tabu. Ms. Maybelline stood over John taking off latex gloves.

"Evening, Reverend." She flashed a professional smile. "He's just had his shot. Maybe he'll be a little more respectful tonight." She bothered the bags and tubes into a rhythmic sway before she left the room.

Mike moved the chair to the side of the bed. In the pale light from the hall, the face on the pillow was all grimace. The skin was pulled tight, the teeth opened in a rigid grin.

At last, John moved his head. "Don't talk." The voice sounded like the rustling of dead leaves. "Wait 'til the stuff kicks in. They give me morphine now. Only four times a day. They're afraid of addiction."

Mike waited.

"I said things I didn't mean," John whispered. "The pain stampedes me. You were furious."

Mike opened his mouth.

"Don't lie, Mike. Not even for piety." John shifted his weight. "Switch on the light and crank up the bed so I can see you."

Mike raised the bed and flipped the wall switch. Shadowless glow filled the room. "That better?"

John's eyes were clear, the pupils dilated. "Turn all the way around."

Mike rotated in place with a silly grin.

"You should get more exercise," John said. "Not bad, though. Large man. Not exactly a hunk, but good looking. If I were well, I'd seduce you. It's in the genes."

"Homosexuality?"

"Good looks. I used to be a large man."

"I wanted more than anything to be big like you." Mike returned to the chair, folded his hands in his lap. "The best time was when you were home, between dinner and going to sleep. No, even better was when I got you to take me swimming and give me rides on your back. Remember the water slide?" Mike laughed.

John's olive-black eyes held Mike in a calm glow, the way they had so long ago. "You were afraid of the diving board."

"Until you held my hand and we jumped together."

"I remember your first head-down dive."

"I went in for competition diving in high school."

John grinned. "Bet you looked good in one of those diving suits."

"I was in great shape. Had to be, all those gainers and swans off the three-meter board." Mike swallowed. "Just before the dive, I'd say to myself, 'This is for Papa.' Later, I got past that. When I finally understood what you'd done—"

John's face lost its smile.

"I loved you," Mike said. "I was happy when you were there. I was alone when you left."

"I had to leave—to survive. I loved your mother."

Mike laughed. "Since when do queers love women?"

John winced. "I was faithful to her until she locked me out of our bedroom—you were five. She had a lover."

"Then you switched to men."

"With relish."

Mike's eyes closed.

"I gave up shame," John said. "Monogamy, too. Until I found Bruce." He dragged his thumbnail across his forehead. "He died first."

"And what about me?" Mike said.

"You belonged to the straight life. I grieved over you. Then I gave up grieving."

Mike shook his head. "So I was left on my own. Who taught me to play baseball? Who taught me to defend myself? I had to learn on my own how to tie a tie, to shave, to drive." Mike bit his lip. "Nobody told me about sex. Nobody taught me to love women."

John froze.

"Nobody," Mike said in a raw whisper, "taught me not to love men."

John's eyes darkened.

"My first time was in high school," Mike said.

"Don't—"

"I swore I'd never do it again. I didn't know how to love a woman, so I knew I had to be celibate or I'd go to hell."

"I don't want to hear—"

"That's why I went into the seminary." Mike leaned his face closer to John's. "I met my first real lover there. I've had every kind of counseling the Archdiocese can think of. Nothing works. It's a curse. Sometimes I think God forgives what you've done but not what you are."

The plastic bags trembled. "Your mother knows?"

"No."

"You blame me," John said.

"You let me grow up alone with the curse."

John jerked up his chin as if for air. "Stop calling it that." The bags shuddered. "You think I chose evil?"

"You blanked me out, forgot I existed."

"Losing you was the hardest part." John drew a slow, deep breath, closed his eyes, and smiled at the ceiling. "'Henry raised both hands before the assembled knights and shouted, "Who will rid me of this troublesome priest?"'"

Mike sat up. "'And the knights there assembled withdrew, saying one to another, "We know the king's will."'"

"You were a tiny thing. I read you history, Shakespeare, Poe, Whitman. On Sundays—you wouldn't remember—when your mom had other things to do, I took you to the ocean. We'd sit in the sand under a buttermilk sky, listen to the rhythm of the waves. You'd sleep in my arms."

Mike took a quick breath. "Yes, *yes*. The beach. I'd forgotten—"

"I tried to forget," John said. "I loved you, more than you knew." He blinked. "But you were better off with your mother."

Pain shot through Mike's chest. It wasn't true. "I want to forgive you."

"You're better off hating me."

"I can't hate and save my soul."

"Bullshit," John said. "Forget 'saving my soul' and 'God's forgiveness' and all the pious crap. Talk to me about living."

"I want to love you."

"Good. You're getting the hang of it."

"Goddam you," Mike shouted. "Stop patronizing me."

"You want to heal your soul, Mike. That's good. Don't muddy the water with ascetic lies."

"My faith was the one thing I've had to hang onto all the years I didn't have you."

John tried to push the tubes away. "Stop whining and blaming. Face the ugliness I gave you. Hate me if you want. But do it without flinching. Then you can talk about religious stuff." He craned his head toward Mike. "Leave the priesthood, Mike. You went into it for the wrong reason. Live for a while. Find out how your body works. And your mind. And your soul. Then go back if you want to. Otherwise, you'll turn into one of those withered celibate lechers who feed on misery."

"My God," Mike said. "My vocation—"

"Mike, listen to me. Life gives you gifts. Took me forty years to learn that they were gifts and another twenty to find out how to use them. Now it's too late for me. But not for you."

"So," Mike said, "first you abandon me, now you want to destroy what I built without you."

"You're not listening." John's head fell back. "I'm getting tired. That's the second phase. After that comes sleep. Until pain wakes me." He straightened his head on the pillow. "After you left last night, after my shot, I remembered those years when you were little. Happy years. I wanted to go back, but I couldn't. Then *you* came back. I thought. 'Mike didn't want me to die alone.' I was kidding myself. You wanted to punish me. I don't blame you. I was fool enough to hope."

John's eyes closed. No signs of breathing.

Mike darted to the bed and put his ear close to John's nose. Breath, faint and sour. He touched the old man's throat. A regular pulse, slow, distant. John's face was already the face of a mummy, skin tight and dry over protruding cheekbones, eye sockets hollow. The eyelids looked out of place, like remnants whose time has passed. The inner corners were wet. Mike bent close. The white eyelashes were moist. He swallowed the hurt in his throat, rested his hand on John's shoulder. Through the hospital gown, he felt bone under stretched skin. He hesitated, then kissed his father's forehead. The bags swung like slowly shaking heads.

The next night, Mike found the room dark. John's face was twisted, his mouth open. He was mewing like a kitten.

Mike took his father's hand. "It's me, Papa."

John groaned. His hand gripped Mike's. "It wasn't my fault. It's the genes."

Mike nodded and squeezed his hand.

"It's not a curse, Mike. It's a gift."

"Yes, Papa."

"Say it. 'Gift.'"

"It's a gift."

John's mouth turned up at the corners. "'Who—'" He stopped, mewed again. "'Who will rid me of this troublesome priest?'"

Mike's eyes watered. "'And the knights there assembled withdrew, saying one to another, "We know the king's will." And they went and found Thomas à Becket and slew him on his altar.'"

"'And when King Henry—'" John's body tensed. He moaned. "'And when King Henry heard the tale, he wept and cried out, "My friend, my friend."'"

Tears blurred Mike's view. "Papa."

"I hurt, Mike."

Mike pushed aside the tubes and took the old man in his arms. "'Ever thereafter, the king mourned. And the people said of him, "Truly this man is forgiven, for he so loved the priest."'"

Best Buddies

Fred eased onto the park bench, short of breath. "Beans, Lulu. We'll have beans. Okay?"

Lulu cocked her head and peaked her ears. Her tail wagged twice.

"I don't want beans, either." Fred bent over, ignoring the pain in his hip, and scratched Lulu behind one ear. With a sigh, he slid back on the bench. Active. Stay active. The doctor said so. "Tell you what. I have a half-price coupon for the Pizza Carousel. How about pizza tonight?"

Lulu wagged her tail.

"Okay. Pizza it is."

The May breeze moved through the beeches and oaks and made the dogwoods curtsey and trail their long flowered arms. They always made him remember how Lisa looked at her first ballet recital. Betty was all proud and grinning. Then Tony wouldn't sit quiet, so Fred had to take him out and missed the second half. So long ago.

Fred gave his head a fast shake. No more of that. The old life was gone. Ended the day Betty left. He filled his lungs with the scent of new growth. Maybe they should head toward the pizza shop at the top of the hill on the far side of the park. No hurry. They'd just stay here as long as they felt like it. They'd eaten lunch less than two hours ago. Hot dogs and canned sauerkraut. Cheap and nourishing. Like beans. *Ah, pizza!*

Lulu danced in place and yipped. Fred heaved to his feet and started down the walk. Lulu trotted ahead, nose to the ground, tail high. Her tawny hair echoed the rhythm of her feet. Half Shepherd and half Collie. Or maybe half Border Collie. The pound didn't know how old she was. All Fred knew was that she was spayed and liked children. And she was beautiful.

They came out of the woods to the softball field with its gentle slope down to the creek. Lulu bounded across the grass, her hair flying. Suddenly she veered, then stopped. She smelled a spot in the grass, splayed her hind legs, and pissed. Fred grunted. Wouldn't life be easy if you could hook up with folks by leaving tinkle messages? Lulu ran on to the far edge of the field, turned, and looked back. He trudged across the infield. As soon as he reached her, Lulu loped on, over the scraggly weeds, through the underbrush, past the playground. A young man with rimless glasses and a tie sat on the bench near the slide. He looked like Clark Kent, all handsome and serious. He was reading some kind of printed document. In the grass beyond the playground, a towheaded toddler in denim bib overalls and a red-and-white tee-shirt stumbled toward the creek. Fred paused. The young man wasn't watching. Then the man glanced up, jumped from the bench, and raced to the child, his tie flying over his shoulder.

"Where you going, Christopher?" the man said. The child grinned, gurgled, and resumed his uncertain steps. The man took him by the hand and walked with him.

Lulu had reached the bridge to the tennis courts. She turned into the trees and ate something. Fred followed her and bent to see. Whatever it was, she'd finished it. "Come on, doggie. Let's head out." He turned back and walked along the creek. The water, blue this time of year, carried pearl-colored dogwood petals and white pollen toward the Anacostia and eventually the Potomac and the Chesapeake, then lost itself in the ocean. Like life, somehow. Made him sad to think about it. Betty had left only a year ago. Seemed longer. He used to call her. Until he understood that she really didn't want to hear from him. She had a new life now. The old life was gone.

Lulu had sprinted on. She ran along the sandy shoreline over rocks and roots and under the leaning trees. Beyond her, Fred saw the man and Christopher. They stooped at the edge of the creek, their hands in the water. The man stood and surveyed the stream, then picked up a stone, hunkered, and threw it side-arm. It skipped three times and landed on the far shore. Christopher lifted a stone and threw it over-hand straight down into the water.

Fred plodded up, a little out of breath. "Want to teach him to skip stones?"

The man laughed. "He's a little young for that."

"They grow up fast."

The man raised his eyes. He was sizing Fred up. "There's plenty of time."

"Less than you think. Before you know it, they're grown up and gone. They have their own children, their own lives."

"Yeah." The man skipped another stone.

"I taught my kids to skip stones," Fred said. "When they weren't much older than Christopher."

The man raised his eyebrows.

"I heard you call him by name," Fred said.

The man stood. "Mike Boynton." He shook Fred's hand. "And that's Christopher."

"Not Chris?"

"Christopher." Mike shrugged. "Don't know why. My wife never liked 'Chris.'"

Lulu had found Christopher. She was nuzzling his crotch.

"Lulu," Fred said.

Mike laughed. "Christopher loves dogs."

Christopher was pulling Lulu's ears. Lulu yelped.

"Easy, guy," Mike said.

Fred squatted next to Christopher. "You gotta be gentle. See?" He rubbed Lulu's head and chucked her under the chin. Lulu wagged her tail, slobbered, and panted. Christopher watched Fred, then rubbed Lulu's head. Lulu licked his face.

"Lulu," Fred said.

"It's okay," Mike said.

Christopher giggled and wiped his face.

Mike ran his hands through Christopher's hair. "You like him, don't you?"

"It's a her," Fred said, getting to his feet. "Lulu. Me and Lulu—we're best buddies. Does Christopher have a dog?"

"No. He lives with his mother. And her boyfriend."

Fred frowned.

"We're divorced," Mike said. "Well, almost divorced."

Fred nodded. "Me, too."

"You have kids?"

"Two."

"Grandchildren?"

Fred grinned. "Four. Oldest is seventeen. Haven't seen the youngest yet. He's eighteen months."

"Christopher's three."

Lulu nudged Mike's crotch, tail wagging.

"Sorry," Fred said. "Dogs don't have no manners."

"It's okay."

"You live near here?"

"Parkview Manor Apartments. High rise. You can see it." Mike pointed.

Fred nodded. This guy had money. "What kind of work do you do?"

"Accountant."

"Is that right? I was a custodial technician for the IRS."

"Small world."

Fred nodded. "How long do you, you know, get to keep Chris?"

"Chris. I like that. You're the first person who ever called him Chris."

Fred shrugged. "Sorry. I slipped. 'Christopher' is a heavy name for a little guy."

"Always wanted him to be Chris." Mike turned to the child, still wooling the dog. "Hey, Chris."

"What time does he have to be back?"

"Eight."

"So you're going to give him dinner?"

"Yeah. We usually hit the fast food places."

Fred pulled out his wallet and fished out the Pizza Carousel coupon. "He like pizza? I got a coupon. Half price." He handed the folded slip to Mike. "Good until the end of May. If you can't use it tonight, maybe—"

Mike unfolded the coupon. "Thanks, but we'll just—"

Fred lowered his eyes. This guy didn't need no half-price coupon. He felt a blush crawling over his scalp. He wiped his mouth and reached out to take back the coupon.

"Hey, that's really nice of you," Mike said.

Fred raised his eyes.

"How about pizza tonight, Chris?" Mike said.

Chris had moved to the other end of Lulu and was pulling her tail.

"Hey, what did the man tell you? Gentle, right?" Mike put the coupon in his breast pocket, knelt in the sand, and moved Chris's hand to Lulu's mane. "Nice and gentle. That's right."

"Me and Lulu have to get going," Fred said. "Nice to meet you. Good luck. Maybe we'll run into each other again."

"Hope so." Mike reached out his hand. They shook. "Thanks for the coupon."

For a moment their eyes met. Then Fred looked away. "Come on, Lulu." Lulu ran back to the walk. Fred followed. He turned to wave, but Mike was skipping a stone across the creek.

As they walked back toward the woods, Fred realized he hadn't even told the young guy his name. He shrugged. "Rice," he said to Lulu. "We'll have rice with our beans, okay?"

Trip Wires

That night in February, the night it all started, Kerney was whooping it up with the usual crowd at the back of the San Diego, home of the shiniest cockroaches, the biggest rats, and the raunchiest whores in Bien Hoa, maybe all of Nam. In the dark of the long narrow barroom, Kerney couldn't tell if his glass had been washed before the girl poured *ba-muoi-ba* in it. He didn't care. He wasn't there for beer. He could almost smell the sweat, piss, and perfume of the cubicles out back where the girls would screw for six hundred piasters if he didn't take too long.

The girl was in his lap, his hand on her breast when the little black guy, Diver, walked in. "Hey, guys, we got ourselves a newbie. Name's Griffin. Griff, this is Hal Riley, the mail clerk. Good man to know. And the runt on the make over there is Tom Kerney."

Kerney looked up. He stopped breathing. Griffin was big and muscular and tanned and blond. His smile was broad and even, his teeth straight and white. His wide-set blue eyes glowed with wonder. Unfinished youth lay like down against his skin.

"Tom?" Griffin put out his hand. Kerney's skin prickled.

"Grab yourself a chair and a chick," Riley said. Diver called to Mama-san for two more beers and pulled up a chair, but

Griffin went on standing, suddenly awkward. Kerney gazed at him. *He's too big for the room.*

"You wan' mo' girl?" Mama-san called back. She waved toward the front of the bar. Four women appeared, chattering. Kerney dumped the girl off his lap, stood, and fought for breath. He sat again, afraid he was going to get the shakes. He beckoned to one of the whores Mama-san had sent them. She moved to his side. He didn't know her. A new girl.

"Sit down, bitch."

The girl glanced over her shoulder toward Mama-san, then up at Griffin.

Kerney slapped his knee. "Come on, baby. Let's see how much you weigh."

She perched on his knee with a sad smile. "My name Rosie." She held out her hand. He took it. Bony and cold.

Griffin was close enough to Kerney and Rosie that either of them could have touched him. The girl named Mary was trying to get Griffin to sit with her.

"You like me?" Mary touched his cheek.

Griffin shrugged and grinned, all foolish.

Kerney could hear Griffin's clothes rustle. He could feel the heat from Griffin's body. He could smell Griffin's musky scent. Looking past Rosie's ear, he could see Griffin's waist and his chest rising above it.

Kerney slid his hand to Rosie's rump. "Come on, baby, relax. Ain't going to hurt you." He pulled her face to him and kissed her. She submitted without response.

"*Shee-it!*" He shoved her off his lap. She collided with Griffin. "What am I supposed to do," Kerney said, "sweet talk you into bed? Hey, Mary, come over here." Mary slithered, sat on his lap, and unbuttoned his shirt. "That's more like it."

"You buy me tea?" Rosie said to Griffin.

"Want to sit at the bar?"

They receded into the darkness. Griffin was too broad to maneuver easily among the close-spaced tables. Rosie moved with brittle grace before him.

"Let's go out back," Kerney said to Mary.

"You pay seven hundred tonight, okay?"

She led Kerney through the smoky curtains. He could barely make out Griffin talking to Rosie at the bar.

Kerney was hung over the next day, but no worse than usual. His memories of Griffin from the night before spooked him. He shoved them aside—he'd gotten into some bad beer or something. As he slurped coffee in the mess hall, he talked with Diver and waited for his stomach to settle. Then he caught sight of Griffin in the serving line. Griffin stood taller than anybody else, his hat tucked into his belt at the small of the back, his blond hair and the back of his fatigue shirt dark with sweat. As he came out of the line, he spotted Kerney and grinned. Kerney swore under his breath, stood, kicked his chair out of the way, and moved to the end of the serving line.

By the time Kerney got back to the table, Riley had taken his usual place next to Diver. Griffin talked on about the night before, about the taste of *ba-muoi-ba*, about the stench of the San Diego, and, finally, about Rosie. "I like her. She's quiet and shy and . . . safe."

Riley paused, fork in mid-air. "Safe?"

"I mean, like, she doesn't want to go to bed. I don't either."

"You got to be kidding."

"It's like this, Hal. I'm married. I, like, don't want to be unfaithful to Anita, I guess."

"Nuttiest thing I ever heard of. Turning down a good piece of ass because of some chick thousands of miles away who won't even know—"

"I'll know."

Kerney narrowed his eyes. What kind of man was Griffin, anyway? Watching Griffin's bent blond head across the table, Kerney hated him.

"Trip wires," Sergeant McCaffery was saying. "Gonna plant 'em. In the ground. Outside the concertina wire. All round the perimeter. So if someone comes wandering up from the river towards our defense, they'll trip a flare, and we'll know they're out there."

"Why not string them in the concertina wire like we always do?" Riley yelled.

"Because," McCaffery said, "we got all that open space between the perimeter and the river."

"What if an animal trips a flare?"

"You shoot it, shithead. And steer clear of the jeep inside the concertina wire."

"Why's it got gas cans strapped in the back seat?" Diver called.

"So's the CO can drive to the coast without stopping for gas, asshole."

Kerney wasn't listening. He was studying the soft, short blond hair on the back of Griffin's tan neck. Griffin sat in the hot sand two rows in front of him, erect, arms folded, watching McCaffery. *Like a good soldier,* Kerney sneered to himself.

"Okay, all you guys got that now?" McCaffery asked. "Then haul ass out there and get them wires in. Come on, move out."

The men got to their feet. Kerney shuffled along with the rest. When he reached the perimeter, he paused, lit a cigarette, and sauntered into the bunker.

"Hey, Diver, how's it hangin'?"

"Too fuckin' hot." Diver looked as hung over as Kerney felt. "Gonna put in to finish my enlistment in the Highlands. Cool up there."

"This one of the new M-60's they just put on line?" Kerney asked.

"Wasn't here last time I pulled guard. They loaded it with tracers so's we can see what we hit at night."

Kerney swung the machine gun on its rest. It responded with oiled ease. Slowly, he turned it toward the jeep. One tracer would blow those gas cans sky high. He swiveled the weapon with studied casualness toward the group of men working in the barren sand on the far side of the barbed wire until he caught Griffin in the sights. Griffin was already stripped to the waist, wet and shining in the burning sunshine. He was lean in the hips and broad in the shoulders. A shadow of hair darkened his chest and ran down his stomach into his fatigue pants. A silver medal on a chain around his neck, next to his dog tags, swung with the motion of his body as he tensed his muscles and forced the spade into the ground. Kerney watched the sight's cross-hairs jiggle at Griffin's navel. He slid his hand to the trigger. Cold and exciting to the touch—wet and slippery from his own sweat. He stroked it with his middle finger. He felt a sudden stab of fierce pleasure. Griffin in the sights, shimmering in the sunlight, big, blond, sinewy.

Kerney snapped the safety off. He caressed the trigger again. Then he shoved the weapon away from him. It clattered back and forth.

"Easy, man," Diver said, now awake and tense. "That motherfucker's hair trigger. You bang it around it'll go off." Kerney gave him the finger and moved out, pulling off his shirt and hat, getting ready to dig next to Riley.

Kerney crouched in the shadow of the mess hall and watched Griffin's wet body bound and spring on the basketball court. He clocked Griffin's regular mail checks with Riley, three times each day. He lingered in the mess hall with Griffin so he could listen to the strange catch in Griffin's voice and feel the resonance of his laughter. He listened as Griffin talked about Anita, the wonderful Christmas they'd shared before he shipped out, and their hopes to have children after he finished his enlistment. When Griffin spoke of Anita, his voice took on an odd huskiness. Kerney wanted to comfort him, to protect him.

Twice, while Griffin was on duty, Kerney slipped into Griffin's barracks and stood looking at his bunk and footlocker, afraid to touch them, but disappointed at how little they told him. The third time he found Griffin asleep on his bunk. Kerney's bowels tingled. Griffin's arm dangled over the side of the bunk. Large hand, larger than Kerney's, a gold wedding band on the fourth finger. Griffin's lips were parted. His hair was matted, and the beginnings of a beard softened the line of his chin. His face had no marks or wrinkles. *He's just a kid.*

Kerney couldn't stop watching Griffin, but he never sat next to him in the mess hall or worked beside him on detail. Up close Griffin suffocated Kerney. Sometimes Kerney had to fight off a desire to reach out to him, to look after him, to ward off things that might hurt him or corrupt him. Sometimes Kerney wanted to hit him and make him bleed. On impulse, Kerney told the girls at the San Diego to seduce Griffin, caress his crotch, unbutton his pants, expose him. Griffin turned bright red, and his eyes filled with angry tears. Kerney felt a shot of searing pleasure. For a moment, just for a moment, Griffin was unmanned, and Kerney had made it happen.

After that, Griffin's trips to the San Diego became less frequent. When he did go, he sat at the bar talking to Rosie. Kerney never saw them slip through the curtains at the back of the bar.

"Kind of odd, sir."

Major Carver, tall and broad, RA-all-the-way in his starched fatigues and polished brass, looked up from the desk and took off his glasses. His question had been casual, to appear friendly, to pass the time while Kerney cleaned the room. Kerney went on sweeping.

"Odd? In what way?"

Kerney shrugged. "Don't know exactly. Guys feel funny around him."

Carver frowned.

"Hard to explain, sir. Just something strange about him. Makes you feel jumpy." Kerney let that sink in. "Way he looks at you. It's like . . . Don't like to take a shower when he's watching."

The revulsion on Carver's face gave Kerney a stab of pleasure in the pit of his stomach.

At morning chow the next day, Griffin was missing.

"Shit," Diver said as Kerney sat down. "The grease trap? Gawd."

"Carver just picked a name out of the hat, and Griff lost."

"Grease trap in the kitchen?" Kerney asked between bites of scrambled egg. "Knew there was one, but I never seen it. "

"You ain't lived." Riley hooted. He folded his hands on top of his head. "Shittiest place in the detachment area, shittier than the shit house. Zip kitchen boy didn't show up, and it's gotta be cleaned, so somebody had to do it. Griff sure has rotten luck."

Pleasure flickered in Kerney's bowels. *Luck, my ass. Carver works fast.*

"Never seen it, either," Diver said.

"Under the floor," Riley said. "Have to take up the tiles. Just a big square tank—maybe four foot by two foot. Three or four feet deep. All the grease and crap flows down there through the pipes from the grills. Gets all full of sludge and stuff."

Kerney stopped listening. He gave himself over to the picture in his head. He saw Griffin groveling and sweating, up to his crotch in grease, filthy, humiliated, degraded. Kerney smiled.

At mid-morning Kerney returned to the mess hall, as if stopping by to get some coffee. He avoided looking at the back of the kitchen until he had greeted the mess sergeant and filled his cup. Then he allowed his eyes to settle on Griffin standing in the grease trap.

Griffin, shirtless, was shoveling out the bottom of the trap with a flat spade. Three garbage cans on a dolly beside the trap were nearly full of gray, rancid slop. He mopped his face with a filthy rag from his back pocket, folded his hands over the spade's handle, and rested his forehead on his knuckles.

Kerney ambled toward the back of the kitchen. He stopped at the edge of the trap. He could hear Griffin breathing. Blotches of sludge and thick sweat dripped from Griffin's forehead. Grease clung to the hair on his chest and under his armpits. The fair hair on his head had turned coarse and shiny with sludge. At the smell of him, Kerney's stomach bucked.

Kerney's pleasure was gone. "Griff?" He bent and touched Griffin's shoulder.

Griffin raised his head. "Don't touch me. I stink."

Kerney lowered his eyes. It wasn't supposed to be like this. "How soon you going to be through?"

"Got to dump this stuff and bury it, then wipe down the trap."

"I'll buy you a beer after you get cleaned up. And if you want, I'll get your mail."

Griffin looked like a little kid. "I'd really . . . like that." He wiped his eyes with the back of his wrist.

Kerney shuffled off, hands in pockets, head down.

"Tom," Griffin called after him. "Thanks, huh?"

Kerney nodded and kept going.

Carver grinned as he read the file. "Phuong thi Xuan alias Tu Phuong, Party name Mai Thang. Born in 1941, raised in Bien Hoa Province, activist in the Viet Cong movement since 1955, Party member since 1964." He slammed the file shut and beamed at Griffin. "Really hit on something, Griffin. This gal is the genuine article. How did you find her?"

"She found me." Griffin flushed at the sudden change in Carver's attitude. "Don't know why she picked me. Told me she was sent to the San Diego to work as a prostitute and pick up information. Told me about it after she found out the Party had beheaded her father. He was our kitchen boy."

"She's the one uses the name Rosie," Kerney said. "Lousy screw. All tense and cold."

Carver laughed.

Griffin looked at Kerney, his eyes wide.

"Is she a good lay for you, Griffin?" Carver asked.

"I only just talked to her at the bar, sir. Bought her tea." Griffin looked at Kerney again.

"She evidently likes you, Griffin," Carver said. "The MI people think it would be better for you to go on seeing her rather than introducing one of their own men into the situation at this juncture. They want you to take her on as a permanent shack job and see what you can get out of her. The San Diego has one-room apartments upstairs, doesn't it?"

Griffin shifted in his chair.

"What's wrong?" Carver asked.

Griffin began pushing the palm of his hand hard against his hair. Kerney had never seen him do that before.

"Griffin," Carver said, "is there any reason why you shouldn't want to make this girl Xuan your mistress?" Revulsion crawled over Carver's face.

"I don't want to cheat on my wife, sir."

"Any other reason?"

"Sir?"

Kerney ground his teeth. *You stupid bastard, tell him about Anita.*

"Frankly, Griffin," Carver said, "your argument does not sound altogether convincing."

"Yes, sir, I know," Griffin said, glancing at Kerney.

"Griffin," Carver began after a pause, "I'm asking you as your commanding officer to go through with this thing despite your—what shall I say—other inclinations?" Griffin blinked. "I cannot and will not command you to do it, and I will try to understand if you refuse. Meanwhile, we don't want to rush things and risk tipping her off. So, even though this matter has come up, I do not plan to cancel the TDY trip to Bo Duc for you, Riley, and Kerney. Think it over while you're gone and let me know."

On patrol in the jungles around Bo Duc, on detail, even during chow, Griffin was silent. Sometimes he sat alone, looked up at the lowest canopy of black leaves, and pushed the palm of his hand against his hair. He drank more beer than he used to, and sometimes he would lurch when he went off to the tent at night. Sometimes when Riley talked to him, he stared into Riley's eyes and then looked off into space again.

Late one dry, hot April afternoon, as Kerney stood guard in his steel pot and flak jacket, he watched Griffin bathe by the stream. Orange sun slanted through the trees and flecked Griffin's tan muscles. Kerney imagined his bayonet piercing Griffin's flat stomach, warm blood discoloring the fine hair.

Riley pulled patrol that night and went off with his squad into the jungle. McCaffery roused Kerney and Griffin before dawn to go in after Riley—he'd been wounded by a booby trap. The VC had dipped a punji stake in toxic juices and splintered the point so that it splayed as it entered Riley's flesh and lodged firmly in the ball of his foot. Every time Griffin tried to pull the stake out, Riley screamed.

Kerney turned away and stared into the darkness. *Riley and that stake are like me and Griffin.* If only Griffin had never existed. Griffin condemned Kerney. Kerney could never be Griffin. He could never possess Griffin. Griffin would have to be gouged out of Kerney like that stake out of Riley's foot.

The punji stake was just the beginning. More booby traps showed up. Riley was medevaced back to Bien Hoa. Hit-and-run raids started. Kerney and Griffin got word to move out. Griffin was ordered out first.

"Here," he said, grabbing his gear and shoving a paper into Kerney's hands. "Give this to company admin before you pull out, okay?"

"What is it?"

"Mail slip. So mail to me will get routed back to Bien Hoa."

Kerney frowned at the rumpled slip.

"Please, Tom," Griffin said, his eyes pleading. "I'm afraid to trust anybody else with it."

Kerney nodded.

As soon as Griffin was gone, Kerney squatted, wadded the slip, and put it before him on the red ground. He took his lighter from his pocket and tested it. It lit the first time. He picked up the slip, clicked the lighter, and moved the corner of the slip into the orange flame. It caught. When the flames burned his fingers, he dropped the slip. He watched it curl and blacken in the red dust. He licked his lips and smiled.

Kerney got back to Bien Hoa at the end of the first week in May. Griffin, with that numb look Kerney had seen in Bo Duc, mumbled that he was shacking up with Xuan. Kerney shook his head and muttered to himself. As if he fucking cared. All he knew was that he was about to explode. He ached to escape to the San Diego, to have savage sex with Mary, but he pulled guard duty the first week and had to stay on base. The following week, all personnel were restricted. One of the guys had been found stabbed to death a block from the San Diego, his penis hacked off and stuffed in his mouth.

On the last night of the restriction, the EM club was jammed, but the beer was good and cold, a lot better than *ba-muoi-ba*, and cheaper too. Kerney sprawled in the sand with the usual crowd out back by the movie screen and drank all he wanted. Griffin sat close by, gazing toward the river, watching in his head some scene that turned his eyes sad in the moonlight. The stack of empty beer cans in front of him rose as fast as Kerney's. The hint of a breeze brushed the hair at Griffin's temples, and he turned his face full to the moon as if listening.

"Hey, kid," Diver said, "got any more pictures of your wife?"

"Let us see 'em, man." Riley, on crutches, gimped across the sand toward them.

Griffin eyed the group, then pulled his wallet out of his back pocket. A string of photos in plastic fell out. Kerney snatched them. The others crowded around.

"These are neat," Diver said. "Sweet little brunette round-eye, you lucky bastard."

"Looks Italian," Riley said.

"Puerto Rican." Griffin turned toward the river again.

"How 'bout that?" Kerney said, warming to the task. "They say them spic girls just love a good fuck." He lowered his voice and leaned close to Griffin's ear. "You fuck her good enough to keep her home nights?"

Instantly Kerney was flat on his back in the warm sand, his jaw stinging. Griffin's silhouette loomed above him against the night sky. His bared teeth glinted.

"Animal," the form said with a voice that made Kerney's hair stand on end. "You shit-eating pig. You prick—"

Kerney got to his knees with Riley's help. "Cocksucker . . . you ever touch me again—"

"Filth, filth, *filth!*" the figure barked. In the moonlight, it looked like a rabid animal, hunched forward, nostrils flared. "You make love dirty. How would you, how would any of you know—"

Griffin covered his face. He was weeping. *Like a little kid. No, like the girls in the bar cry sometimes.*

"Stop it!" Kerney got to his feet. "Jesus, I'm sorry. Christ, kid, please stop that."

Griffin was lurching away from them.

"My God, my God," Kerney said.

"You're bleedin', man," Diver said.

"Why did he say that to me? Can't stand him to be like that."

"It's not you," Riley said. "He hasn't gotten no mail for two weeks." He kicked the sand with his good foot. "Just hate to see him come to mail call. He gets kind of sick looking, you know?"

Carver stood before the map in the operations Quonset, studying Griffin's squares and arrows around Tuy Thanh. Kerney sat, hang-doglike, saying nothing. Griffin, taut, pressed his hands on the gray desk top and stared at the reflection of the fluorescent light in his wet palm prints. The air in the room waited, tense.

Carver shook his head. "Why should they want to launch a sapper attack against our outpost at Tuy Thanh? There's not one stitch of corroborating evidence."

Griffin tightened. "Like I said, sir, they're handling the whole thing as top secret. The attack command won't be issued until the last minute. Even the sapper unit commander hasn't been told the target."

"And you believe her?"

"Yes, sir. She . . . I think she's in love with me."

Carver looked hard at Griffin. "How would you know?"

"Sir?"

"How do you know she's in love with you?"

"She just acts like it, I guess."

Carver continued to watch him.

Griffin shifted. "And she says she loves me."

Carver threw up his hands. "Any whore in Bien Hoa will tell you that."

Griffin didn't answer. He just sat there, head lowered, opening and closing his hands on the desk top.

"Suppose," Carver said, "just suppose that General Hackel buys it. And imagine for the sake of argument that he decides to send a relief force to Tuy Thanh. Could you find out from her the current disposition of their forces in the area, whether they could ambush a relief column, what kind of communications they have, whether they have the means to forewarn the sapper unit that we're coming? Could you ask her without letting her know what you're up to?"

"Wouldn't need to trick her, sir," Griffin said. "She'll tell me. She'd do anything for me."

"Even betray the VC?"

"Yes, sir."

Carver hesitated. "All right. Find out as much as you can tonight. I don't for a moment think that General Hackel will believe this story, but the possibility that it's true is serious enough that I must make him aware of it." Carver reached for the telephone. Kerney and Griffin rose together and walked out of the Quonset into the white heat.

"Why does he hate me?" Griffin said.

"Just trying to do his job."

"And I'm trying to do mine. God, God, God—"

"Easy, kid. Back off. Don't take it so serious."

Griffin laughed, and his body jerked. *Don't*, Kerney wanted to say, *please don't jerk.*

"Kid, let's have another beer before chow. Cool you off."

"Got to check the mail."

"Skip it tonight."

"Can't. Got to go check."

Griffin was waiting for Kerney just outside the gate. Without speaking, they turned toward the San Diego. They walked side by side. Kerney fell in step with Griffin.

Once inside the bar, they separated. Kerney headed to the back. He sloshed down *ba-muoi-ba* after *ba-muoi-ba*. When he lost count, he took a girl to the back—he couldn't see who—but his cock lay dead between his legs. He went back to drinking. He raised his eyes to the ceiling. Griffin was up there somewhere destroying himself for Carver. Kerney imagined Griffin's lion-body with Xuan beneath it and gagged.

A hand shook him.

"Tom. Quick. Help me get wheels."

Griffin dragged him to the street. They flagged a vespa to take them to the base gate. "I'll call from there," Griffin said. "Carver'll send a jeep."

When they reached Carver's quarters, Griffin was flushed.

"Changed their target, sir. They know we're on to them. They figure we've sent our strike force to Tuy Thanh, and we won't be ready for a surprise assault here, on our own perimeter. There's still time. Xuan says they can't be in position on this side of the river before two in the morning."

"But I've told General Hackel they're on their way to Tuy Thanh," Carver said.

"I know, sir, and that was the plan. Xuan will be dead by morning." Griffin's voice faded, and his eyes fluttered. Then he rallied. "Even without calling back the relief column, we'll have enough men here to beat off the attack if we get them to the perimeter before the VC hit. We have almost an hour—" His voice died under Carver's glare.

"What kind of bullshit do you expect me to swallow?" Carver said. "You honestly believe that I'm going to call General Hackel at this hour and feed him a tale like that? I can't tell if you are lying to me, or if she is lying to you—maybe feeding you what the VC want us to believe. Or, for all I know, the VC are lying to her, because they know she's passing it on to you. Use your head, Griffin. Do you think me so naïve as to believe the Viet Cong would attempt to mount a sapper attack against this base?"

Carver turned away and waved them from the room with a sweep of his hand.

Kerney started out, head down, fighting the knots in his stomach. At the door he stopped. Griffin was standing still, head cocked, staring at the back of Carver's neck. The muscles in Griffin's face sagged. Sweat dripped from his chin. Kerney darted back, took Griffin by the shoulders, spun him around, and pushed. Griffin stumbled at the doorway, but Kerney caught him under the arms and kept him moving.

In the moonlight, Griffin stood limp. Kerney twitched in front of him.

"Kid, you okay?"

Griffin's eyes focused. He closed his mouth and swallowed. His face came to life. Tears filled his eyes, and he began to chuckle. The chuckle turned to laughter, tense and hollow. He dropped to his knees and doubled over, convulsed in gales of laughter, then wrapped his arms around his head and pushed his face into the sand.

"Stop it," Kerney cried. "Griff, it was my doing, don't you see?"

Racked with laughter, Griffin shoved his face deeper into the sand.

Kerney knelt beside him. "It's over, man." His arm went around Griffin's quaking shoulders. His heart contracted. "Griffin." Tears started down his cheek. "Griffin."

Griffin raised his head. Kerney pulled away and fell backwards on the sand. Griffin peered toward the river as though listening. He was panting. "Tom!" He looked hard at Kerney, then looked toward the river again. He sprang to his feet and yanked Kerney up. His eyes glowed. "Tom, there's still a way. I can stop them. I can scare them off. I can bring the whole goddam U.S. military force to the perimeter." He gazed toward the river once more and smiled. Still panting, smeared with sand and tears, he turned full face to Kerney. "Tom. My friend. You stuck by me."

He let go of Kerney's shoulders and stepped back without taking his eyes from Kerney's face. Then he bolted.

Kerney watched the blond figure lope through the night. "No." He ran after Griffin. "No, Griff. No."

Griffin got to the perimeter first. He snatched an M-16 from the guard on duty, dashed to the jeep inside the concertina wire, started it, and smashed through the perimeter fence toward the river. Flares fired as the jeep hit trip wires. Before Kerney reached the bunker, the guard shot more flares into the air. They burst, high above, and bathed Griffin and the bounding jeep in orange light.

"Griff, come back here, you bastard!" Kerney screamed.

Griffin kept going. He called toward the river as more flares burst over him. Thirty yards out, he slammed on the brakes, leaped to his feet, and sprayed the shoreline with fire from his M-16. Then he roared forward, stopped again, stood, and fired. Roused by the shouting and gunfire, the detachment came to life.

Kerney stood watching it all happen as if it were a soundless movie in slow motion. The screaming inside him drowned out everything else. He was sobbing, out of control. "Goddam you, Griffin. Goddam you, goddam you, goddam you." Then no more words, nothing but screaming.

He shoved the guard aside and swung the M-60 toward Griffin. He fixed the jeep's strapped-on gas cans in the sights through a blur of tears and squeezed the trigger. The weapon shuddered. Tracers flew from the barrel to the jeep vaulting over the grass and sand. The cans exploded in a burst more beautiful than any Kerney had ever seen. Through the smoke, the burning figure standing in the jeep tilted and fell to the ground, limbs askew, like a broken marionette.

Fuchsias

Jane looked up at the pots of fuchsias hanging on each side of the front door. Full and lush, trailing large red-and-white blossoms and dark green leaves, meticulously trimmed and perfectly balanced. No sign of die-back yet. That would come. By this time next month, the plants would be wilting in the heat. Bill had watered them this morning, within the past few minutes. She could almost feel his presence as he pushed back the tendrils and nourished the roots. He handled these plants with the same care he showed when he helped Sarah fix her bike or Jenny braid her hair.

But he wasn't here now. Where had he gone?

She heard a shout from the backyard. Touch-tackle—the midshipmen along with Jenny and Sarah... Mother's Day. Thirteen mids here to celebrate. They'd come early from the academy to surprise her. And Bill disappears. How could he agree to sponsor the mids, offer them a home away from home on weekends, and then hide when they show up?

She went back into the house, stepped into the bathroom off the hall, closed the door, and studied herself in the mirror. A motherly presence? She hoped so. She was, after all, old enough to be the mids' mother.

She smoothed her hair, freshened her lip gloss, and turned to the side to get a glimpse of her profile. She reached for the hand mirror and stopped. Bill's shaving mug was gone. His toothbrush was gone from the holder above the sink. She opened the medicine chest. His razor gone. Maybe he'd finally decided there was no need to shave and shower in the downstairs bathroom. Or maybe . . .

A flicker of panic. His talk about moving out. Like his mood swings. For the last year, she could almost time the season by them. Every three or four months he withdrew and got crabby. There'd be talk of separation. Then, after a week or two, everything was fine again. Friday night, before any of the mids arrived, she'd asked him please not to ruin the weekend. And here he was, missing. Maybe not. Maybe he was somewhere in the house.

She left the bathroom and walked through the family room. The kitchen door was closed. She pushed on it. It was bolted from the inside.

"Hey," she called.

Laughter inside. Some of the mids were in there.

"You can't come in," a young male voice said.

Of course. Mother's Day. They were fixing her breakfast. She'd eaten long before they arrived, but she'd go along with the surprise.

"Don't take too long. I want a cup of coffee. Bill in there?"

More laughter. The door opened and Tommy's hairy arm held out a cup. "Haven't seen him."

She laughed and took the cup. The door closed. She heard the bolt slide shut. She smiled. What a mess they'd make. Bill would clean up after they left for the academy.

She opened the French doors leading to the patio. From the steps, she watched the game on the back lawn. The group had divided into two teams. Jenny was on one and Sarah on the other. Sarah had the football now and was running the length of the yard screaming her head off. The mids faked attempts to tackle her as she reached the flower bed and held the ball up in triumph.

"Sixty-seven to sixty" a voice cried. Sarah giggled and tossed the ball to the nearest mid. As she stepped from the flower bed, she left mashed petunias behind her. Jane scanned the lawn. Gashes in the grass here and there. Even though she'd asked them to play barefoot. Bill wouldn't say anything, but he'd be out there tomorrow night with grass seed. He'd buy more petunias.

No sign of him out there, either.

She went back in the house. She glanced into the dining room and the living room. No Bill. Maybe upstairs.

A cheer from the back of the house as she climbed the stairs. Jenny must have scored. Jane opened the bedroom door.

On the bed were two suitcases. The open one held folded suits and starched dress shirts still wrapped around cardboard from the cleaners. Undershorts and balled socks were tucked into each corner. She felt the panic again.

She heard him in the dressing room. Another shout from the back yard. She stepped to the open window. Sarah stood beaming in the petunias.

Bill came through the door from the dressing room dressed in khaki shorts and a button-down sport shirt. He carried stacked tee-shirts and the picture of Sarah and Jenny from his desk.

"What are you doing?" she whispered.

"Moving out." He went to the bed and arranged the clothing and picture in the suitcase, then closed it. "I told you I was going to. Don't think you believed me."

"They'll hear you."

"Does it matter, Jane?"

"What brought this on?"

"Same-old, same-old."

She set her coffee on the end table and sat on the bed. "What's your complaint this time? The shape the house is in? Sponsoring too many mids? Not enough time with the kids? Not enough cuddling?"

"For Christ's sake, Jane. Cuddling? Can't you bring yourself to say the word, sex? Say it. Sex." He cupped his hands on both sides of his mouth, faced the window, and yelled, "SEX!"

"Shh!" She went to the window and looked down. The game was going on. Their yelling had drowned out his. She turned back. "I don't know why you're always finding things to complain about. We have a nice home, good jobs, two fine daughters. A nearly perfect life—"

"Designed to impress others. But inside, nobody home."

"We have a good time together."

"The girls and I have a good time. You and I don't."

"That's your opinion."

He sat on the bed, folded his hands in his lap, and looked at them. "My opinion. Does it matter? I fulfill my role. I cut a respectable figure. The cardboard husband in the cardboard family."

She glared at the suitcases. "Seems what I want doesn't carry much weight." Her eyes went to the window. "How do you think I feel? You get moody. You withdraw. The mids are here, and you're nowhere to be found. It's mortifying."

"Sorry, Doll. Some things are more important than the mids."

"Don't call me Doll."

A shout and laughter came through the window. Then talking. The game must be over.

"I need to get downstairs," she said.

"Don't let my departure delay you."

"Stop talking about leaving!"

He stood. "Why don't you throw a scene? Smash dishes. Break windows. Holler until you're hoarse."

"Please don't talk so loud."

He looked at her, his eyes round, his mouth solemn, and tipped his head toward the window. "There's your world, Jane. Go to it."

"Don't leave," she said. She felt tears coming. "I didn't think you meant it. I thought you were trying to scare me."

He laughed. "You mean you're finally taking me seriously?"

"I always take you seriously. I love you."

He gave her a controlled smile. "You love me."

Yes, she loved him. She didn't know how to make him see that. She loved his cowlick that never stayed combed. She loved his poker-face one-liners. He was the home she came back to at the end of the day. He was her comfort, her peace.

"Jane?" a voice called from outside. It was Tommy. "You out here?"

She bustled to the window. "Up here."

Tommy, standing on the patio in one of her aprons, turned and looked up. "There you are. Have any powdered sugar?"

"What on earth for?"

"Military secret."

"In the cupboard next to the refrigerator."

Bill was sitting on the bed, his face in his hands. She touched his shoulder. "Don't leave, Bill. We love you, Jenny and Sarah and I. We need you." She sat next to him. "I don't know what's wrong, but I'll work with you to make things better."

He shook his head. "The speech. I knew it was coming."

"What do you want me to do?" she cried, then glanced at the window. "How do you want me to change things?"

"Don't think you can change. Don't think you see what's important."

She shook her head. "I can't do therapy. I just can't."

"I know. To go into therapy, you have to want to change."

"What's wrong with that? I'm happy. *We're* happy."

"You're happy," he said.

"Then maybe you're the one who needs therapy."

"I tried that."

She ground her teeth. "Maybe it didn't work. Try someone different."

"And embarrass you again?"

"Just don't talk about it. Don't tell everyone."

"Will you come with me?"

She shook her head. "I see no reason for it."

He nodded. "No reason." He took a deep breath and started toward the dressing room.

"Bill—"

"Jane?" Tommy again. On the stairs this time. Jane wiped her face with her hands and hurried to the bedroom door. "Yes?"

"We can't get the mixer to work. Plugged it in and turned it on and nothing happens."

"Turn on the wall switch."

"Any chance Bill could give us a hand? Lot of stuff we can't find."

Bill shook his head.

"In a bit, maybe," she said.

She closed the door and leaned her back against it.

Bill went into the dressing room and came out carrying his workout bag. "Why don't you just tell them I'm leaving?"

"And ruin their surprise? Bill, we have our ups and our downs, but there's no need to take it out on the mids."

"No need at all."

"What do you want me to do?" she cried softly. She went to him and put her arms around his neck. "Don't do this to me!"

"Then start paying more attention to Jenny and Sarah. Take time off to go to Parents' Day. Sign them up for swimming lessons this summer."

"The only slots left are on weekends. I'd have to drive them. I wouldn't be here for the mids."

"Then tell the mids to go away."

She felt herself redden. "And where would they go? How could they get sponsors for the summer?"

"That's their problem."

"It's *our* problem. We can't just cut them off."

"We might have a fighting chance as a family without the mids."

"So unfair of you, blaming the mids."

"I'm not blaming them. I'm blaming you, for Christ's sake." He spread his arms. "Before the mids, it was the church folk group. Before that it was garden club. Before that—"

"You want me to do nothing but work and sleep? I *need* the stimulation of other people."

"You need the adulation of other people."

"So now," she said, "the truth comes out. You're jealous of them, aren't you?"

He cocked his head. "Guess I am, at that."

"So it *is* your personal problem, isn't it? You can't stand the attention I give others."

He nodded. "That's one way to look at it."

"That's crazy, Bill, just plain crazy. Don't you see that?"

"I see it."

"For God's sake, be reasonable," she said louder than she meant to. "What in the world do you want me to do?"

He put his workout bag on the bed and looked at her. "Make love to me. Tell them all to go home and then let's go to bed and make love."

"You're insane."

"Probably. You asked what I want. That's what I want."

"Hey, Jane?" Tommy's voice on the stairs. "Come on out back. We're waiting for you."

She started toward the door, then wheeled. "Do you have any idea how unreasonable you're being? Any idea at all?" She laughed silently. "I think you need help."

"I think I need help, too."

"Jane?" Tommy called.

"Be right down," she yelled through the door.

Bill looked tired. He took a deep breath. "You want me to tell them to leave? Then they wouldn't blame you—"

"*No!*" she yelled, then covered her mouth. "I just don't know what's the matter with you," she whispered. "Why can't you behave rationally?"

"Then I'll just tell them I'm moving out but to go on with the party, okay?"

"*Stop it!* You'll ruin everything—their big surprise, their Mother's Day—

"Your Mother's Day."

"Yes. My Mother's Day! What have you done to celebrate it? What have the girls done?"

"You haven't looked in the living room? A present from Sarah. And roses from Jenny."

"Why didn't you tell me?"

"They're a surprise."

"Hey, Jane," several voices shouted from the stairs. "Come on."

Bill sighed. "Guess I'd better be on my way."

"Please, wait until tonight. Until after the mids have left. We'll talk."

She stepped to the vanity and peered into the mirror. Her face was a mess. She wiped it with tissues, then dabbed on some powder and brushed it away. Her hair had come loose. She shaped it with her fingers, sprayed it lightly, and wiped her hands. She gave Bill one last pleading look, then hurried to the door, down the stairs, and into the hall. At the door to the living room, she hesitated.

"Jane!" a chorus of young male voices called.

She passed through the family room, through the French doors, to the patio. There on the picnic table stood a cake, frosted in white, lit by more tiny candles than she could count.

"Happy Mother's Day," Tommy said. "Happy Mother's Day," the others repeated. She felt tears coming. "Jeez," Tommy said with a frown. "We hoped you'd like it, not cry."

"I *do* like it. I'm so touched." Jane sniffed and wiped her eyes. "You made this yourselves?"

"Yep." Tommy grimaced. "We'd better eat it. The frosting is sliding off."

A gap had appeared on the side of the cake. The candles were starting over the edge.

"Make a wish and blow them out," someone said.

She leaned down and blew. Most of the candles went out. She blew a second time and got the rest of them. The mids cheered.

She heard the front door open and close. She looked back through the French doors. She couldn't see anyone in the hall.

"Just a second," she said with a smile and started up the steps.

"Hey," Tommy said, "aren't you going to have some cake?"

She turned back. "Of course."

Tommy beamed and cut her a piece of cake. A shattering sound from the front porch. Then another. She looked toward the doors.

"Try it," Tommy said. "We want to know how it turned out."

She cut a bite with her fork and put it in her mouth. Sugary. Probably not done. "Wonderful!" she said. "Now you all have some."

She heard a car start. It was backing down the driveway. Panic bubbled in her stomach.

"Just a minute," she said. "Be right back."

She dashed up the steps, through the family room, through the hall, out the front door to the porch. Bill's car was just turning the corner at the end of the block.

"Bill!"

The car disappeared. She was panting. She turned to go back in. As she did, she tripped. She looked down. Fuchsias. The hanging pots. Dirt and broken blossoms and leaves and mangled stems and pottery shards.

Trembling, she stumbled back into the house. She went into the bathroom and closed the door. The mirror told her she was a mess.

"Jane?" she heard Tommy call from the hall. "You all right?"

She practiced her most gracious smile in the mirror. It looked good.

"Fine," she said. "Fine."

Jolly, Jolly Sixpence

After Riley and Joey had scrubbed the metal plates from Riley's old Army mess kit, a souvenir from Nam, they settled by their campfire.

"I brought you a little something," Riley said. "Early birthday present. You can use it tonight." He fished in the knapsack until he found the olive green Army flashlight with the head turned at a right angle to the body. He'd tied blue plastic ribbon around it.

Joey took the flashlight, tried it, set it in the dust beside him.

"You know that weeping cherry tree in front of the house?" Riley said. "I planted it the day you were born. So your birthday is, like, its birthday."

Joey kicked at the fire.

"Don't do that, son. You burn your new sneakers, your mom'll have a fit." Riley handed Joey a long branch from the kindling pile. "Here. Tell you what. I'll teach you a camp song I learned from an Aussie in Nam. 'Jolly Sixpence.'"

Joey poked the fire with the limb.

"You're always supposed to sing by the campfire," Riley said. "When you're old enough to go camping with the Boy Scouts—"

Joey wiped his nose on his wrist.

"Use your handkerchief," Riley said. "Is something the matter?"

"Were you what they call a casualty in Vietnam? Mom said you were hurt."

"What's eatin' on you, son?" Riley asked.

"It's just, um, I can't go camping two weeks from now."

Riley swallowed. "How come?"

"Mom wants you to switch weekends with her. She wants to do something, you know, special for my birthday." Joey threw a twig into the fire. "She said you'd be mad."

"I'm not mad."

Riley kicked a smouldering log further into the fire. *Jesus.* That Saturday was supposed to be *his* weekend with Joey. They'd agreed that he'd get Joey every other weekend.

"It's no big deal," Riley said. "We'll celebrate late, that's all. Like we did at Christmas. I'll get a cake and we'll have candles and everything around the campfire."

Sunday morning, while they were packing, Riley found the flashlight by the dead campfire, its ribbon intact. He dropped it in the knapsack. Before driving Joey home, Riley canceled the reservation for two weeks from then. He couldn't get anything for the weekend after Joey's birthday. The campground, the best in West Virginia, was booked through September. Trouble was when Joey stayed with Riley in the apartment, Riley had to sleep on the floor so Joey could have the sofa bed.

Sure enough, that night as Doris stood with the storm door open and the heavy wooden door closed behind her, she asked him to switch weekends. "He can't be with you this coming weekend, either. Swim team try-outs. We'll move everything up one weekend and in the fall you can have him two weekends in a row, okay?"

"I'll swing by on his birthday and give him my present."

"Don't do that," Doris said quickly.

Riley frowned.

"The party's up at my mom's" Doris said. "Our backyard's, you know, so small,"

"I'll bring it by Friday night."

"We're going up Friday morning, staying the weekend."

Riley told them he could work the Saturday of Joey's birthday, but they'd already scheduled a full crew. They even had someone to pump gas while the regulars worked on cars in back. Riley was left with nothing to do. That morning, he scrubbed his hands and did the best he could to wrap the green-and-white box that Joey would instantly recognize as swim fins. The finished package looked pretty bad. The blank side of the wrapping paper showed at the creases, and the ribbon was barely long enough for a knot on top. Joey wouldn't care. His mom had told him fins were just too expensive, so he wasn't expecting them. Maybe the next time they went camping, the fins would put Joey in a better mood, and Riley could teach him the sixpence song.

He was half fish, that kid. Riley had to watch to be sure he didn't go out too far. When he was littler, Riley kept him in the shallows by giving him horsey rides. He sat on Riley's shoulders while Riley pranced waist-deep and listened for Joey's giggled commands. At the end always came, "Throw me, Daddy." Riley would lift him straight up and fling him into the deep water. Riley chuckled. He could still hear Joey's screams of laughter.

That was before the divorce. Joey was different now, almost like he was afraid or didn't trust Riley. Had Doris told

Joey about Riley's nightmares and the couple of times he'd gotten kind of wild? That was all past now. Mostly. The VA's counseling had helped.

With nothing better to do, Riley washed several days' worth of dishes. Dishwater got the dirt out of the cracks in his skin and loosened the grime under his fingernails. As he put the last dish in the drainer, the old refrain jostled through his head. *I've got sixpence, jolly, jolly sixpence.* A bum's song. No money, no responsibilities.

I've got sixpence to last me all my life.

He and Doris had enough money before the marriage went sour. Of course, she made more than he did. They didn't care. They had each other, their little house, their baby. He hunched over the edge of the sink. Swaths of grease floated on the surface of the brown water.

I've got tuppence to spend . . .

Even with the cut they'd given him, Riley'd paid almost a hundred dollars for Joey's cherry tree. It hadn't bloomed much while Riley was living at the house—too young. But when he'd taken Joey home from camping two weekends ago, the tree was fully budded, its limbs touching the lawn. Should be full out by now—on Joey's birthday. And Joey wasn't home to see it.

Riley shook his head and dumped the dishwater, cleaned the sink, and swept up. In the living room-dining room-bedroom, he considered making the bed and folding it back into a sofa. Instead, he tossed his pillow on top of the twisted sheets.

Tuppence to lend . . .

He sponged the plastic tablecloth, took his *Penthouse* from the coffee table, and flipped on the floor fan. Up in the eighties already. He dreaded the onset of summer heat and the daily decision about how much air conditioning he could afford. He'd try to get through the hot days with shorts and tank tops.

Tuppence to send home to my wife, poor wife.

He opened to the centerfold. Doris hadn't asked for alimony, but he'd insisted. That plus child support. They'd agreed that she'd only pay him a quarter of the house's value—when she had the money—because she'd paid the mortgage out of her salary, and he'd paid for groceries and utilities and kept the place up.

No cares have I to grieve me . . .

He turned pages. Overblown bodies flashed past his eyes. Beautiful spring day. He should get out and get some exercise. He stood long enough to crank open the window. The ground in the U-shaped apartment complex was strikingly green in the patches where grass still grew. The scrappy forsythias were out and forgotten daffodils up. He'd love to see his and Joey's cherry tree—well, not *his* anymore, but he'd planted it and mulched it, fed it, protected it against the worst of the winter freeze. It was nearly fifteen feet tall now. Maybe he could drive by sometime when Doris and Joey were out and sneak a look.

No pretty little girls to deceive me . . .

Springtime. Supposed to let your fancy turn. Lots of babes hung out at Clyde's on Saturday nights. Maybe some pub crawling would help him chase away the blues. Wouldn't cost much if he stuck to beer and drank slow. He'd been hiding out long enough. Time to get out and howl.

Not tonight.

I'm happy as a lark, believe me . . .

Riley pushed the magazine away. Another bad day. If he didn't watch it, he'd end up on a crying jag. He stared at the phone. Doris wouldn't be at the office. She'd be at her mother's. With Joey. Riley knew he shouldn't do it, but he so wanted to hear her voice. He lifted the receiver and dialed her private line at work. After the second ring, the recorded announcement came on.

"This is Doris Riley at the Landgrave Institute. I'll be in on Monday. Leave me a message, and I'll get back to you."

Doris had a little girl's voice, in keeping with her small, perfectly formed body. He pictured her gray eyes, her short dark hair swept back on the sides and a swag over her forehead. Ears like newly opened roses. He could see her in her fitted business suit and black pumps. Serene, poised. Doris had never been needy. She'd gone with Riley because she wanted to be with him. Then, one day, she didn't want to anymore.

Happy as the day when we line up for our pay . . .

Damn, he was misting up. He stepped into the kitchen and grabbed a Kleenex. Maybe he could get out for a while, do something. Doris and Joey weren't home. He'd drive over and leave Joey's present inside the storm door and see the cherry tree.

As we go rolling, rolling home.

With Joey's present safely belted in on the passenger side of the pickup, Riley drove the mile and a half. Flowering trees and jonquils were everywhere. Spring was going all out this year. The perfume of freshly mowed grass, new blossoms, the living earth swept through the pickup's open window. By the middle school, he headed in, two rights, and he was there. He slowed to five miles an hour as he approached the house at the end of the cul-de-sac.

On the far side of the cherry tree, heavy with bloom, Doris's blue Chevy was in the driveway. Behind it was a huge black pickup with four floodlights above the windshield and a vanity plate that said "BLACKBOX." Riley pulled to the curb two houses away.

Doris was unloading groceries from the truck. A tall, athletic man, graying at the temples, handed her brown paper bags. Joey bounded from the front door and across the lawn. The man laughed and handed him a cake box. Joey reverently carried it into the house. Doris waited until Joey was out of sight then said something. The man grinned and pulled a green-and-white pasteboard box from a plastic bag. *Jesus.* Swim fins. Doris laughed, took the plastic bag, and went into the house. The man got the remaining groceries, closed the cab door, and strode across the lawn, up the stairs, and into the house. The storm door closed behind him.

Riley was panting. He snatched paper towels from the roll on the dashboard and blew his nose.

The storm door burst open, and Joey tripped down the stairs. He ran to the pickup and stopped. The man appeared on the porch, laughing, and called to Joey. "That's all, son." Joey started back. The man met him in the middle of the lawn and scooped him into his arms. "I'll give you a horsey ride." He swept Joey over his head and onto his shoulders and mounted the steps. Joey giggled. Doris opened the door from the inside, smiling. Joey hugged the man's head and laid his cheek against the long hair. The man lowered Joey to porch, and all three went in.

Sweat poured from Riley's scalp, around his ears, down his neck, into his eyes. A breeze rustled the trailing flower-covered arms of the cherry tree. Petals blew across the grass. Riley shuddered.

He released the emergency brake, pulled a U-turn, and found his way past the middle school to the main drag and eventually to the apartment. In the parking lot, he turned off the ignition and stared at the carbon-singed brick façade, the cave of an entrance banked by mailboxes, stairs barely visible beyond them. He'd always known that Doris was too beautiful to remain alone. He'd steeled himself. But Joey. . . *I'll give you a horsey ride.* Joey's laugh. His hug. Riley slammed his eyes shut and banged his forehead against the steering wheel.

Still shaking, he carried Joey's present across the parking lot to the garbage cans and tossed it in.

Inside the apartment, the air was lifeless. He opened the window and turned on the fan. How long until dark? Five hours. He knelt by the table and rifled through the tool crate. The hatchet would be useless. The tree's trunk was too thick. Maybe the bow saw. He fingered his chainsaw. He'd have to get gas and check the oil, be sure it would start right away.

For the rest of the afternoon, he sat in the apartment and watched the shadows lengthen. He'd have to wait until it was completely dark. Maybe Doris would forget to turn on the porch light. He'd park around the corner and hope nobody recognized his pickup. He'd have to be quick, before anybody figured out what he was up to. He'd try the bow saw first. If that didn't work, the chain would cut through the trunk in about ten seconds. Then he'd kill the saw's engine and be gone before anybody saw him. He'd use his knapsack to carry the bow saw. He found Joey's flashlight still in the knapsack.

At sunset, he drove to the gas station, changed the chain-saw's oil, and filled its tank. In the vacant lot next to the station, he worked with the saw until it started every time he pulled the cord. He spread a camping tarp over the pickup's passenger seat, laid the saw on its side, and folded the tarp over it. It reminded him of the way Joey looked when Riley put him to bed. The knapsack fit on the floor with room to spare. He'd have to drive gently to keep the saw from falling off the seat. Back in the apartment, he stared through the window at the fading light.

As darkness fell, he forced himself to wait. It must be completely black. Clear sky. There'd probably be a moon. Never mind. The mature oaks and maples at the end of the street would cast shadows. He dressed in his old fatigues and boots and stuffed a bandana in his rear pocket.

By nine, convinced it wouldn't get any darker, he slipped out of the apartment and drove slowly and quietly. Before the final right turn into the cul-de-sac, he parked, took the chainsaw and his knapsack, and slid silently from the truck. No one on the street. Lights inside the houses. Families cleaning up after dinner. A television flickered in a window. As he turned the corner into Doris's street, he stopped. A dog was barking frantically. Of course. The Milligan's mutt. Barked every time anybody went by their place. He'd quiet down as soon as Riley was past.

Down the street to the yard. He paused in front of the neighbor's place. Doris's car and the black pickup were still in the driveway. Porch light on. *Damn.* Lights on in the living room and Joey's room. Didn't provide much illumination close to the street. The moon was brilliant but blocked by the tall trees. The street lamp. *Shit.* He'd forgotten about the street lamp across from the house. He'd have to be quick and quiet.

He darted to the cherry tree, knelt, and pushed away the weeping limbs. By the light of the street lamp, he gauged the thickness of the trunk. He started the cut with the bow saw. Six inches above the ground. A quarter inch in, he wiggled the saw out. Sap poured from the wound. The sharp sweet tinge of pitch filled his nostrils. He stopped, looked, listened. No sign anyone had seen him. He resumed his sawing. Rough going. Pitch clogged the saw teeth. He worked the saw out, wiped the blade and the tree wound with his bandana, forced the saw back into the cut. No good. It was going to take too long. He eased the saw out, again wiped its blade, and put it into the knapsack.

He pushed the chainsaw's sprocketed blade against the cut. He'd wasted time. Should have cut with the chainsaw in the first place. He dragged the teeth and chain against the wound in the tree and grasped the pull-cord.

A shaft of light from the porch fell across the lawn. The front door was open. A small figure stood inside the storm door. Joey in his pajamas, peering into the darkness. Doris came into the doorway behind him. They opened the storm door.

"See?" Doris said. "There's no one out here."

The tall man stood beside Doris. "What's the matter?"

"Joey thought he saw something."

Riley crouched beneath the blossom-covered tentacles and held his breath.

"Okay, sweetie?" Doris said to Joey.

She let the storm door close, took the man's hand, and disappeared. Joey frowned into the night.

Riley kept his eyes on his son. The image of the boy in the doorway went blurry. Riley was crying. With as little motion as possible, he slid his free hand into the knapsack and felt for Joey's flashlight. His finger snagged on the bow saw. He felt blood and pitch on the ribbon and flashlight's slick plastic casing as he pulled it from the knapsack. He dropped it silently to the ground and put his finger in his mouth. The metallic taste of blood dulled the flavor of tree sap.

Still watching the tear-smudged figure in the lighted doorway, Riley yanked the chainsaw pull-cord. The saw roared to life and shattered the silence. He trained the blade against the cut in the trunk. The chain sliced instantly through it. Riley switched the saw off. The Milligan's dog was yelping hysterically. The tree trembled, leaned, and began a graceful descent. It gained speed as it fell and bounced when it hit the lawn, its arms fluttering.

Joey screamed.

Riley locked his throat and held the hurt in. He felt for the bandana with his free hand and mopped his eyes until he could see. With the knapsack over his shoulder, he picked up the chainsaw, and walked across the sidewalk. The dog was going crazy. Without hurrying, Riley headed down the middle of the street, turned left at the corner, got into his truck, and drove to his apartment.

Rolling home, rolling home, by the light of the silvery moon . . .

In the kitchen, he washed sap and blood from his keys and took a beer from the refrigerator. He cleaned the saws and put them away, stripped to the skin, and dropped the knapsack, the bandana, and his clothes into the dirty clothes basket. Sipping beer, he shaved and brushed his teeth. In the shower he scrubbed the last of the sap from his skin. After he'd bandaged his finger, he put on clean jeans and a fresh tee-shirt, combed his hair. Action in the bars didn't start until eleven. He had plenty of time. On the way out the door, he dropped the *Penthouse* in the trash.

Happy as the day when we line up for our pay
As we go rolling, rolling home.

E-Square

The day Tuohy's father died, I learned a whole lot.

Laurie called me at work at ten in the morning. I dropped everything and took off without even telling them I was going. I had to be with Tuohy. I took the Metro out to the Silver Spring station where I park my car and drove like a crazy woman, half crying, half scaring myself to death, around the Beltway to College Park.

As I sailed under the bridge at I-95, all I could think was, poor guy. His father was all he had. I'd known Tuohy my whole adult life, for almost twenty years. Of course, I didn't tell people that. I'd kept my figure and used lots of moisturizer with alpha hydroxy, so I didn't look that old. Tuohy did, though. He spent all his time in bars, even when he wasn't working. He had flecks of gray in that wiry brush on his head he called his hair, and his beard had more gray than brown. Still, he looked pretty much the same as he always had. Shaped like that football player they used to call "The Refrigerator," square and huge, except that Tuohy had a belly on him. Behind those glasses, though, you saw the big brown eyes, soft like a puppy's.

Off the Beltway onto the Route 1 access road.

I'd given Tuohy his nick name. Must have been more than fifteen years before, Wendy and Kurt and Laurie and Tuohy and me were hanging out at Louie's. Tuohy was hitting on this girl. She couldn't get his name, so I said, "Like Two-E. You know, like E-E?"

She looked him up and down and laughed. "E-Squared."

That cracked us all up, and he's been E-Square ever since.

He got back at me, though. Another night a few weeks later, Mark walked up to me and introduced himself. I said my name was Trish.

"Or Trash," Tuohy said. "As in Trash-mouth."

I fisted him in the gut. He laughed, but my hand hurt.

Route 1. Turn south.

Mark. So long ago. We went together three years before I wised up. He got his kicks by smacking me around—nothing that ever left bruises—and I was dumb enough to put up with it. At the end, he was tired of me and left me pregnant.

Tuohy took me to the clinic and brought me back and helped me upstairs to my room in this shared house I was in. He got me into bed and took care of the cats and brought me cold stuff to drink. While I slept, he sat in a kitchen chair next to the bed. When I woke up the next morning, Tuohy's big brown eyes, all blood-shot, were watching me.

"You okay?" he said.

Took me a while to find my voice, but I finally said, "Yeah."

He hunched his shoulders and nodded. His cheeks were wet.

We'd gone out, Tuohy and me, right in the beginning when I was waitressing at The Cavendish. I served early bird specials and lots of bland food and fried fish and Salisbury Steak. Tuohy was the evening bartender, on the same shift as me. After two dates, Tuohy asked me out again, but there was no chemistry. We stayed buddies, though, always checking out people for each other. I was the one who sicked Tuohy onto that girl who called him E-Squared.

Left on Erie. Only a couple of blocks to Tuohy's street.

Chemistry between me and guys was a complete mystery. I sure had it for Mark and a few others. It wasn't the way the guy looked. It was, like, the way he touched me or maybe the sound of his voice.

Anyway, I didn't trust chemistry anymore. I used to wish I could be like Laurie. Only a week before Tuohy's father's death, we'd been in Robbie's Sports Bar, and Laurie was there with Chick. They had this machine where you put in quarters then tried to pick up dolls and teddy bears with these remote tong type things. Tuohy and Chick both nabbed stuffed animals. Tuohy got this cute little red and white cat and gave it to me—"Add it to your cat collection." He knows how I am about cats.

Chick snagged a yellow kangaroo and gave it to Laurie, and she got all teary. Tuohy and Chick laughed at her and went back to the machine, but I sat at the table with her because I knew it was for real. She wiped her eyes and got mascara on her cheek and blew her nose. "I've had two boy friends, I mean *real* boyfriends, before Chick. God, I hope this one sticks." And then she went to the ladies' room to fix her makeup.

I understood. Guys like to go from girl to girl, but a woman wants to find someone to spend her life with. Laurie never paid a whole lot of attention to how *she* felt about guys. She just wanted them to care enough to stay with her. I couldn't be like that. I always had to feel something about a guy, at least in a, you know, chemistry way. I'd gotten pretty cynical. Tuohy said I sent out "don't touch" signals. All I knew was here I was pushing forty and it'd been a long time since any guy spent more than a minute or two with me at a bar.

The sad part was that I always wanted more than anything to end up with a guy I really cared about. I remembered that night wishing I had someone like Chick, and I heard my mind say "to grow old with." Kind of shocked me.

Wendy and Kurt and Laurie and me had all moved up, career wise. When I saw that waitressing wasn't ever going to net me much, I got into lab work. I'd been at the GWU Hospital for twelve years and worked days. I moved to an apartment in downtown Bethesda, a little above my budget, but I skimped on other stuff, so me and my cats could make it.

Tuohy hadn't gone anywhere. He lived in his father's house, a little rancher in College Park. He'd moved back to take care of his father when his mother died, so he never needed a lot of money. Maybe that's why he stayed a bartender.

Tuohy's street. I almost missed it. All these strange cars were all over the place. I finally found a parking place a couple of blocks up and ran back. I rang the doorbell, and this grey-haired lady with red-rimmed eyes let me in. Turned out she was Mr. Tuohy's sister. She thought I was a medical person or something—I still had on my lab coat. I asked for Tuohy and she said sit down, she'd get him. He was still with his father's body. She got me settled, then went down the hall toward the bedrooms. I could hear and half see a couple of other people talking quietly in the kitchen. All I could get was something about "funeral" and "showing."

Tuohy came schlepping down the hall. I'd never seen him like that before. He had his eyes down, and his head was tilted to the side. When he came into the room, he stopped and gave me the saddest look I've ever seen. Then he started crying. He stood there, arms hanging loose, tears rolling down his cheek into his beard. I knew he wasn't just crying for his dad. He was crying for his whole life, being alone, not having anything, no future, all the sad stuff we usually laughed off. He couldn't fight it anymore. So he cried and cried.

I went over and leaned my head against his chest and put my arms around him. I wanted to tell him it was all right, but it wasn't. So I held him. For the longest time we stood there with our arms around each other, his tears dripping into my hair, mine wetting his chest.

I didn't want to let him go. When I saw him so hurt and helpless, I couldn't take it. I never wanted to see him hurt again.

We're still together, Tuohy and me. And my cats.

Some things are more important than chemistry.

The Song of the Earth

Limpy—her real name was Olympia for the doll in *Les Contes d'Hoffman*—was seventeen. The pound had listed her as "mixed breed." Luke guessed she was part collie, part shepherd with maybe some golden retriever tossed in. Her red fur, once silky, was coarse and tufted like desert grass. She moved slowly these days and, like Luke, had a terrible time with stairs. Her eyes were milky from cataracts, and she was so deaf that Luke had to use exaggerated hand signals to get her to obey. She got disoriented and forgot where she was. And yet she was still beautiful.

Jeb, the young singer Luke coached three times a week, laughingly called her Luke's Portrait of Dorian Gray—all Luke's problems showed up in her. Luke had to smile. He'd had cataracts removed, depended on his hearing aids (a real curse for a musician), and controlled his arthritis with ibuprofen. His brain still worked, though, except for occasional forgetfulness, of course. But, then, there were things he wanted to forget.

"I don't know." Jeb watched Limpy resting at Luke's feet under the piano. "Maybe you should think about having her, you know, put to sleep—"

"I won't have her killed," Luke said, "as long as she can enjoy living."

69

Jeb gave his head a slow shake, still watching her. "All she does is eat and sleep and do her business."

"Wrong. Come with me sometime when I take her to the park. She sniffs and hunts and looks and listens."

"She can't hear anything."

Luke gave Jeb a patient smile. "She hears the song of the earth."

Jeb blanked.

"I mean," Luke said, "she hears life with her inner ear, like I'm always telling you to do."

"The inner ear. A vintage Luke-ism."

"Something every singer has to have. If you'll pardon me, my young friend, yours is still a little on the tinny side." Luke smoothed the pages of the piano score and adjusted his glasses. "Back to *Kindertotenlieder*. 'O du,' all in one breath to the D flat—"

Jeb marked his own score on the music stand in the curve of the piano.

"Then," Luke said, "carry the whole next line, two and a half measures to the first B flat, on a single breath."

Jeb marked.

"The most important thing, Jeb, is to hear the anguish in that line. Hear it in your heart. Then let your voice show what you hear."

Luke cued Jeb in with two bars before the voice part. The hearing aids turned the notes shrill in Luke's ears. By habit he adjusted the sound in his mind.

When they reached the B flat, Luke sighed. "Sometimes I think a man without children . . . I wish you hadn't insisted on *Kindertotenlieder*. You've never lost a child. You—" Luke's voice stalled. He blinked and swallowed.

Jeb hadn't noticed. He scratched his head. "I can't get the hang of it."

Luke straightened himself and played the voice line with no accompaniment. "Listen, listen, listen. If I didn't know you had it in you, I wouldn't be working with you. Listen with your heart."

After Jeb left, Luke took Limpy to the park. She dragged along after Luke. When he stopped, she stopped. He led her along her favorite trail, away from the macadam walks and bike paths, through woods thick with oaks and beeches, to the edge of the creek where the filtered sun splattered across the rollicking water. As she came from under the leaf canopy into the mottled sunlight, she stumbled on the rocks and fell on her side with a yelp. Her legs grabbled in alarm.

Luke stooped beside her with a wince, rolled her to her stomach, and ruffled her fur. "Having a bad day, aren't you, girl?"

She lowered her head to her paws and rested her chin. Her cloudy eyes were grim.

Panic shimmered in Luke's belly. Limpy wouldn't live forever. He knew that. Maybe this was a temporary setback, like others they'd been through together. He waited until she could walk and then headed slowly toward the apartment, pausing to let her rest. When she was settled on her mat in the studio, he gave her a pain pill. Maybe she'd snap out of it.

She didn't. The next day he gave her a double dose. She slept. When she awoke, he couldn't coax her to the kitchen for her dinner. He brought her dish to the studio and put it on her mat within inches of her nose. With her chin on the floor between her paws, she raised her eyes with a look that said, "I hurt."

Luke, on his knees, scratched behind her ear. "Don't do this, Limpy. You can't give in. You've got to get going, girl."

Her eyelids dropped closed.

"Don't," Luke said. "Please don't."

She was quiet except for uneven breathing.

He'd give her one more day. Then he'd get Jeb to take them to the vet. She had to spark up.

When he went to bed that night, Limpy didn't follow him to the bedroom. He couldn't carry her. He left her where she lay in the studio. Once during the night she cried—a long guttural howl. He checked her. She seemed to be asleep. She was breathing.

During Jeb's session the next day, Luke wasn't at his best. He'd cleaned the accident Limpy'd had and opened the windows. He hadn't been able to get her to take another pain pill. She hadn't eaten. She lay in the same spot, on her mat by the bookcase, her eyes sometimes open, sometimes closed.

Luke tried to concentrate. He adjusted the score and struck an A flat. "Same place," he said to Jeb. "Mahler wrote this line so high for a reason. He wanted the strain to show in the voice. It's one of the few places in the whole cycle when anguish breaks loose. Listen to the hurt in the accompaniment. Read the words, 'O you, o you, your father's heart, the light of happiness, so soon extinguished—'"

His eyes watered. He couldn't speak.

"You all right?" Jeb asked.

Luke fumbled for his handkerchief. He blew his nose and wiped his eyes. With an apologetic glance at Jeb, he turned toward Limpy. "She's only a dog."

"What?"

"Will you help me take Limpy to the vet? With my arthritis, I can't lift her."

At the vet's, Luke told the receptionist it was an emergency. Doctor Gunther, a large jovial woman with a long face and ample mouth, guided them to the closet-sized examining room. Jeb eased Limpy down on the aluminum table. Luke shuffled along behind.

Doctor Gunther lifted Limpy's head and studied her eyes. "What's the problem?"

"She's been like this for two days," Luke said. "She was fine Monday."

Doctor Gunther cooed to Limpy as she listened to the dog's heart and worked her limbs.

"She's deaf," Luke said.

Doctor Gunther gave Luke a quick smile "I know that, Luke." She rolled Limpy over and felt her stomach. Luke tensed, but Limpy only whimpered.

For twenty minutes, Doctor Gunther prodded Limpy, listened to her heart, peered into her ears and mouth, and finally gave her a rectal examination. She stripped off her latex gloves, washed her hands thoroughly, and sat in one of the folding chairs. "Let's talk." She patted the chair next to her.

Luke maneuvered himself into the chair. He hadn't taken his ibuprofen. Jeb stood by the table, his fingers stroking the top of Limpy's head.

"I can't tell what brought it on," Doctor Gunther said. "Might have been a stroke or heart attack. When you're that old, it can be anything."

"What can you do for her?" Luke said.

Doctor Gunther took a deep breath. "She's seventeen. It's miraculous she's lived this long, a dog her size."

"Maybe a stronger pain killer—"

Doctor Gunther shook her head.

"Last time," Luke said, "the steroids worked. Snapped her right out of it."

"I don't think—"

"Even a change of diet. We don't have to worry about fat at her age. If I could get her to eat—"

"She's dying, Luke."

Luke opened his mouth, then closed it.

"She's in pain," Doctor Gunther said. "She could drag on like this for days."

"No," Luke said. "I can't—"

"Let me put her to sleep."

"*No.*"

Luke squeezed one hand with the other, as if to warm up before playing. He darted glances around the room.

"You want to take her home in the shape she's in?" Doctor Gunther asked.

Jeb put his hand on Luke's shoulder. "You could wait outside. I could stay with her while Doctor Gunther, you know—"

Luke couldn't hold still. His leg jiggled, his hands wandered over his shirt, searching.

"Why don't you both go on home and leave her with me?" Doctor Gunther said.

Luke raised his eyes and started to speak. He had no voice. He looked down, folded his hands carefully, cleared his throat. "She's only a dog."

They watched him and waited.

"Let me hold her," Luke said, "while you do it."

Doctor Gunther nodded and stood. "I'll be right back."

Jeb stepped out of her way.

"Will you bring her to me, Jeb?" Luke said.

Jeb slipped his arms under Limpy. She groaned low in her voice. He lifted her gently and hunkered in front of Luke. "Ready?"

Luke spread his arms, palms up. Limpy was a dead weight in his lap. "I don't have a free hand," he said to Jeb. "Pet her. Comfort her."

Luke scratched the top of her head.

"It's okay, Olympia," Luke said. "I'm here. We'll do this together."

Limpy forced out a wail.

Doctor Gunther, in a long white apron and fresh latex gloves, came in with a razor and large syringe. She sat next to Luke. "Turn toward me so I can get to her."

Luke twisted, careful not to disturb Limpy.

"She won't feel anything," Doctor Gunther said.

She shaved a small spot on Limpy's leg, removed a rigid rubber covering from the needle, and pierced Limpy's flesh. Limpy raised her head and turned it toward Luke. Her foggy eyes questioned him. Doctor Gunther pushed the plunger slowly and evenly and withdrew the needle.

Limpy's muscles tensed. Her eyes widened. Her haunches thrashed as though she were struggling to her feet. She opened her mouth, and a long deep groan filled the room. She shuddered, then flopped, her muscles loose, and lay still.

"I'm so sorry," Doctor Gunther said. "I should have anesthetized her. Every once in a while—"

Luke's heart was beating so hard he could see the pulse in his eyes. "Jeb, take her and put her on the table."

Jeb scooped Limpy from Luke's lap. Her head and legs hung. He slid the body on the table and looked over his shoulder. "You all right?"

Luke nodded and clasped his fluttering hands. "Just give me a second. It's all right, Doctor Gunther. I know these things happen. You did a professional job. Thank you."

She looked relieved.

Luke and Jeb wrapped Limpy in an opaque black plastic garbage bag. Jeb carried her to his car and laid her on the rear seat. They drove by Jeb's place for a pick and shovel, and then to the park.

"I'll show you where," Luke said.

He carried the tools, and Jeb carried Limpy. They moved through the trees, along Limpy's favorite path, away from the walks and bikes and baby carriages and runners, to the creek.

"Here," Luke said.

Jeb squatted and let the bag slide onto the creek bank. "You know this is illegal."

"I know."

Jeb took the pick.

"It has to be deep, Jeb, so other animals won't find her."

Jeb dug. The ground was rocky. It took almost an hour. Jeb took off his tee shirt and wiped the sweat from his body.

"Deep enough?" he said.

Luke looked into the hole. Three feet deep at least. "I think so."

Jeb scrambled from the hole, mopped his face, and put his shirt on. He picked up Limpy and climbed into the hole. "You want to leave her in the bag?"

"No."

Jeb laid the body on the ground at the bottom of the pit and offered Luke his hand. Luke clenched his teeth against the pain in his legs and struggled into the hole. Together they tugged Limpy from the bag and arranged her on her side so that she looked comfortable. Luke tried to close her eyes. He couldn't.

They covered Limpy and filled the hole. Luke lumbered back and forth over the shoveled dirt to level it. When he was through, it still formed a mound.

"We can sort of mulch it so it won't show so much," Jeb said.

Together they gathered fallen leaves from the woods and spread them across the mound. Luke found dead limbs and twigs and scattered them over the grave.

"That's good enough," Jeb said. "No one will notice."

Luke leaned on Jeb on the walk back through the woods. He yearned for ibuprofen.

"You want to rest for a minute?" Jeb asked when they came to the meadow and picnic tables at the edge of the woods.

They sat side by side in the shade. Luke rested his elbows on the table and massaged his cheekbones.

"You okay?" Jeb asked.

"Thanks for today," Luke said. "We'll schedule a make-up session to work on *Kindertotenlieder*."

"Glad I could help." Jeb stirred the grass with his toe. "Have any plans for dinner?"

Luke shrugged. "Limpy and I were going to have left-over pot roast."

"The Peking Palace has a daily special."

Luke shook his head.

"You going to be all right?" Jeb asked.

Luke raised his eyes to the boughs above them. "Funny how the loss of an animal can bring back old hurts. She was only a dog."

"You should get a pup."

Luke nodded. "I'll start over. You can't give up. Limpy never did. Until she had to." He tried to smile. "I'm getting deafer and deafer, but I can still hear in my head."

The sun was low in the sky.

"Getting late," Jeb said. "You ready to go?"

Luke looked at the sky. He listened carefully. His hearing aids distorted the sound of the breeze through the trees, but he could still hear it. He smiled. "Yes."

Wolf Rock

When life stumped Charlie, he retreated into music. That's what he wanted to do now. He stood fidgeting in the feathered shade of the cedars at the edge of the creek and sniffed the sun-splattered earth. Water breaking over the rocks struck five distinct tones, the first three and fifth and sixth pitches of the B-flat scale. The sound reached his ear in random variations, never the same order of tones, never the same rhythm, patterns blurring into patterns. He closed his eyes and shook his head. *There you go again. Admit it. You're stumped.*

From behind him came the *plink plink* (F-sharp) of Boyd pounding in tent pegs. Boyd, his beautiful son, was so unlike Steve, his strong son, that sometimes Charlie wondered if their mother, Evelyn . . . *Don't get off on that.*

He meandered back through the trees, ducking low beech branches heavy with June's fresh growth. Ashes from campfires lit for countless years in this spot greyed the red Maryland earth. The smell of burned wood, male sweat, and the untroubled Catoctin forest made him grin. He saw dirty feet and skinned knees and pint-size swim suits hung on limbs to dry. They'd started coming here when the boys were little because it was the only vacation he could afford. They'd never stopped.

Once past the clearing where Boyd, cross-legged and bare-foot, was tapping in the last stake, Charlie stopped by Steve's car, a rented candy-apple red Thunderbird. Sweet car. He opened the door to his own '83 Ford pickup of no particular color and took his acoustic Martin from behind the seat. He sat on the folding chair by the camp table and plucked.

Boyd looked up and smiled. The Bible had it wrong. It should have said, "It is easier for a camel to go through the eye of a needle, than for a beautiful man to enter into the kingdom of heaven." Boyd *was* beautiful. Too beautiful for the word "handsome." He was tall and angular with the kind of grace that always made Charlie think of an eagle full to the wind, yet thick enough from working out that his body was manly. His hair, eyebrows, and eyelashes were the color of tarnished brass, his skin just tawny enough (granted, from sun lamps) to look robust, his wide-set eyes a May-sky blue.

Charlie picked a slow B-flat scale and compared the tones to those from the creek. His relative pitches were truer, but he'd tuned a hair sharp. He damped the strings and blew the air from his lungs. This wasn't getting him anywhere. What was he going to do?

When he'd gone by the efficiency apartment that morning to pick Boyd up, Boyd had apologized. "Sheila didn't have time to clean up before she left. Told her I'd take care of it."

But he hadn't. Charlie ignored the dirty coffee cups, a saucer with the hardened residue of Timmy's soft-boiled egg, a milk glass, and a cereal bowl on the dinette. The kitchen floor was sticky.

"Sheila took the car?" Charlie asked.

Boyd fumbled for an answer. "Yeah, she did." He stepped over shoes into the closet. "That way she can head back whenever she wants. Where'd I leave my boots?"

"What did Sheila tell them at work?"

"Whatever." Boyd emerged with the boots and gave Charlie a grin that made the whole room shimmer. He sat on the bed and unlaced the boots. "Grab my keys from the work table."

Charlie found the table behind the electronic keyboard, the amp, the speakers, and a music stand shedding its hand-written manuscript sheets to the floor. Wires ran from the amp to the guitar laid across the table. He pawed through the dust on the table's surface, through scraps and sheets and pens and pencils and guitar picks. No keys. Beneath the guitar and a stack of manuscript paper, gritty to the touch, he found a stack of envelopes. The top one, from Potomac Electric, was stamped in large red letters, "FOURTH AND FINAL NOTICE." Under it an envelope from MasterCard. "OVERDUE" was printed in blue above the address. Six or seven other bills were beneath the first two. None had been opened.

Charlie strummed a B-flat chord and frowned up through the cedar branches to the darkening sky. Boyd and Sheila were in trouble again. Charlie was still in debt from the last time. Had Boyd told Steve? Not likely. Charlie laid the Martin on the camp table. Decision made. He didn't know where he'd get the money, but he couldn't allow Boyd to go through bank-ruptcy.

Steve, all muscle and hair, came huffing out of the woods carrying more dead limbs and branches than Boyd could lift. He dropped them next to the fire pit and mopped his forehead with his bandana. "Think this'll be enough?"

"It'll get us through breakfast," Boyd said.

Charlie poked through the woodpile. "Need kindling. Boyd—"

Boyd pulled on his boots.

"Don't get your hands dirty," Steve said.

Boyd gave him the finger. "I'll wear gloves." He disappeared into the woods.

Charlie broke a limb over his knee. "Quit trying to pick a fight."

Steve dragged a branch to the pit. "He's the smart ass."

"He's got big problems right now."

"Boyd always has big problems."

"Lay off him."

Steve dropped the branch by the pit. "He's always taking advantage of you. I get pissed."

"He's not taking advantage."

"Where did he disappear to when it was time to pay for the gas? Where was he when we were in the grocery store?"

"He's between gigs. Doesn't have any money."

"And his credit's shot. And another baby on the way."

Charlie dropped the limb.

"Didn't tell you, huh?" Steve said. "Sheila's due in October. The Starlight doesn't like their cocktail waitresses to look pregnant. Let her go. You going to bail him out again?"

Charlie stood straight. "None of your fucking business."

Steve leaned a limb on the stone by the pit and stomped. With a loud crack, its upper half went flying. He moved the limb up and stomped again.

"Look," Charlie said, "the whole idea of this trip is to let Boyd unwind for a couple of days while Sheila and Timmy are in Philadelphia."

"Thought it was so Boyd and me could spend some time together while I'm east. That's why I rented the car and followed you up here."

"That, too."

Steve took a beer from the cooler and slumped at the camp table. "Dad, when are you going to stop running interference for him?"

Charlie reached for a beer and sat next to him. "He's my son."

"So am I."

"You did fine. You're hardheaded. A loner. Like your mother."

Steve laughed. "So the one who did fine gets yelled at."

"You've got no complaints coming."

"It's just that he—" Steve took a slug of beer. "I feel ashamed for him."

Charlie stood so fast that his beer fell over. "*Ashamed?*"

Rustling and swishing. Boyd came through the trees dragging a large, dead limb. "This'll be plenty when we break it up."

While Steve got the fire going, Charlie opened the spaghetti can and dumped it into a scorched pot. Boyd improvised chords and riffs on Charlie's guitar. Soon he was singing softly over a repeated pattern of three chords.

"What's that?" Charlie said.

"New tune. Trying to get the bridge to work."

Charlie started coffee. Same three chords—D, E, A— in the bridge. Same key. Only the melody was different. Then the refrain came back. The song ended with a coda that sounded like an afterthought.

"What's it called?" Charlie said.

"'Freedom Rock.' Like you always taught us. 'Go for life. Go for love. Don't sell your soul for money.'"

"Nice work if you can get it," Steve said.

Boyd went on playing.

"Steve's got a point," Charlie said.

Boyd stopped. "That's not what you used to say."

"Never was able to live up to my own philosophy. Always wanted you boys to have things better than I did."

Boyd strummed an A, then damped the strings with his palm. "I never understood why you settled for so little after

Mom left. Why didn't you just say 'fuck it,' play music, and have a ball?"

"And let you boys starve?"

Boyd started playing again. Same three-chord pattern.

"What're the words?" Charlie asked.

Boyd strummed an intro of eight bars, four-four, then began the refrain.

When you've had it up to your neck with the nine-to-five,

And you can't see your way out of the tunnel,

When you wake up at dawn not sure you're alive,

And your life's being forced into the corporate funnel,

The time has come, my friend, to run free.

It's none too soon, my friend, to run free.

'Fore death comes 'long, my friend, run free.

Boyd played the three chords twice more and stopped. He looked at Charlie.

"Nice," Charlie said, stirring the spaghetti.

Boyd cleared his throat and stood. "I'll set the table." He put the guitar back in the pickup and laid plastic forks and paper napkins on the camp table. Charlie spooned the spaghetti onto paper plates.

As they sat down, Steve smiled. "Spaghetti."

"Guess I'm set in my ways," Charlie said. "Cheap and healthy. Like camping."

"Haven't eaten spaghetti since I got married," Steve said. "But I take the kids camping. They love it."

Boyd's smile faded. "I used to love it."

Charlie picked up his fork. "Not any more?"

"Not when everybody's getting on my case."

"Steve's got your best interest at heart, Boyd," Charlie said.

Boyd shrugged. "Maybe. I don't see it his way. The daily routine isn't for me and Sheila."

Charlie nodded and ate a forkful of spaghetti. "I know how you feel. But—"

Boyd tightened. "But it keeps the wolf from the door."

Charlie put down his fork and stared at his plate. "Maybe you should set some limits. Maybe you should say, 'Okay, I'll give it another five years. If I don't make it by then—'"

Boyd grunted. "Jesus. You, too?"

"You've been at it almost twelve years, Boyd," Steve said. "Maybe it's time to get it out of your system."

Boyd pushed his plate away and sat back. "I'm just not a desk jockey. I'd suffocate." He ran his hand through his burnished hair. "You don't understand, Steve. Some things you can't get out of your system. Ever since the first time I saw Dad play and saw all those people watching him like he was magic or something, ever since then, I've had this vision of being up there with the lights and the mikes and the sound equipment and my group behind me. And then the crowd going crazy." He wiped his mouth with the back of his hand. "You never had dreams like that."

"How do you know?" Steve said. "I had them, all right. But not the same as you. I saw myself building computers and trackers and radars and missiles. I saw myself with a nice house and a woman I loved and kids who would run out in the yard every night when I got home and yell, *'Daddy!'*" He finished his last mouthful of spaghetti. "I worked my ass off to make it happen. Had to do it by myself."

Charlie winced.

Boyd sipped his coffee. "It's not the same. Right, Dad?"

"I don't know, Boyd," Charlie said. "I can't see inside either of you. I can only see inside myself, and not too clearly at that."

"What did you want?" Boyd said.

"Something sort of like you. I wanted to bury myself in music, eat it, dream it, sleep it. But when your mother left, I learned that sometimes the people you love are more important than your dreams." Charlie swallowed the last morsel of spaghetti. "Selling shoes pays the rent."

Steve gave Boyd an I-told-you-so look, then went to the fire and poured them coffee. "You have any health insurance?"

Boyd shook his head without looking up.

"Sheila have any?" Steve said.

Boyd shook his head again.

"How're you going to pay for the baby?"

"Goddamn you, Steve," Boyd said.

"I told Dad," Steve said. "Why didn't you?"

"I was going to. While we're up here." He gave Charlie a quick look. "Baby's not due until fall. By then, I should have a regular set of gigs."

"And if you don't?" Steve said.

"I can do some modeling."

"Thought you said they were looking for young kids."

"I can always go back to waiting tables."

Steve spat. "How the hell are you going to make enough to pay the doctor and the hospital and the lab fees and anesthetist—"

"That's enough," Charlie said. "We didn't come up here to fight. I told you to quit picking on him."

Boyd put their plates and napkins in the fire. He dumped the forks in the garbage bag, then looked at the sky through the trees. "Getting dark. Want to sit down by the creek with our coffee?"

Charlie awoke to the sound of the creek scolding in B-flat and birds chattering polytonally in the trees. When he opened his eyes he saw the roof of the tent dim above him. He turned his head. Boyd was asleep on his stomach, his arms embracing his pillow, his hair falling over his face. Steve's sleeping bag was empty. Charlie struggled to his knees and found his clothes. He crawled from the tent on all fours, stood upright, stretched his unwilling legs, and sat on the log to put on his jeans. The sharp blue of the sky told him the sun was above the horizon. He knelt by the creek, splashed water on his face, listened to the rapids, then shuffled to the fire pit. A small fire was burning. A pot of coffee sat on the rocks.

Steve came through the trees with a load of logs in burlap on one shoulder. He wore dark slacks and a button down, long-sleeve plaid sport shirt with creases still in the arms and chest. He let the logs fall into the woodpile.

"You're all dressed up," Charlie said.

"Thought I'd get things started for you guys before I shove off."

Charlie's stomach clenched. "You leaving?"

Steve nodded. "The kid's driving me crazy."

"Stop calling him *the kid*. He's almost thirty."

"Someone's got to level with him."

Charlie swallowed hard. "Barely had any time with you. You flying out Monday? Why the hell can't you two get along?"

"He makes me ashamed."

"Stop it." Charlie turned to the fire pit.

"Come see us after the baby's born," Steve said.

Charlie shook his head.

Steve put his hand on Charlie's shoulder. "I'll pay for it."

Charlie tried to speak, but the lump in his throat stopped him. He closed his eyes.

"Love you, Dad."

Steve's hand left Charlie's shoulder. Footsteps, then a car door. An engine started.

Charlie's chest hurt. He'd let Steve down again. It was just that—Charlie kicked the dirt. Steve could always take care of himself. Boyd couldn't. When Evelyn left, Boyd needed a lot of help. Steve just got real quiet. Went off by himself all the time. Steve had been on his own since he was ten.

He had the sausage cooking by the time Boyd stumbled from the tent in his boxer shorts. He sat at the table and pulled on his jeans. Charlie poured him coffee.

"Where's Steve?"

"Headed back early."

Boyd nodded and sipped. "I'd like to hike up to Wolf Rock."

"Suits me."

As the sun climbed and the heat of the day settled on the earth, they trudged up the trail that looped back and forth across the eastern side of the mountain. They made their way over roots big as Charlie's wrist, around boulders that would have dwarfed the pickup. Toward the top, the trees grew thicker, the leaves greener.

"Got anyone to look after Timmy while Sheila's in the hospital?" Charlie said when they were finally able to walk side by side.

"Me."

"None of my business, Boyd, but how are you paying the doctor?"

"Sheila's folks."

"Jesus."

"I always figured," Boyd said, "that by the time we had another kid, I'd have made it. But this one sort of took us by surprise."

Charlie took a deep breath. "Got anything in the works?"

"Looked like Cheap Thrills was going to take me on to play bass. Fell through. Guess I can still play once at week at the Starlight. Except in September. They've already booked. I've been looking into doing the sound set-up for other groups."

Charlie was surprised, as always, how Wolf Rock appeared out of nowhere just beyond the wall of oaks and ashes. "Want to go to the top?"

Boyd grinned. "Don't we always?"

Boyd climbed first. Thirty feet up, he disappeared onto the long flat top of the formation. Charlie followed him, pulled himself over the edge, and stood. The uneven and broken top of the rock table extended a hundred feet to their left and fifty feet to their right.

"Why do they call it Wolf Rock?" Boyd said. "Sounds like a song title."

"You always ask that. I don't know. Guess there used to be wolves up here."

Boyd laughed. "The first time you told me that, you scared me to death. I expected to find a wolf around every corner." He clapped Charlie on the shoulder. "But I knew you'd protect me."

They turned left and walked along the expanse of rock. As they approached the end, they stopped and looked in all directions.

"Steve left because of me?" Boyd said. "Steve just doesn't get it. He's no artist."

"Keep your mouth off Steve."

Boyd's eyebrows went up and his mouth opened. He pursed his lips and shrugged. "Sorry."

"Want to eat?"

They went back by a different route, as they always had, down the steeper path on the western side of the mountain.

Hot, tough going. The trail was steep, embedded with worn, slippery stones. Trees were wide spaced and small, symptom of the forest fire here some years back. By the time they reached Jeopardy Rock half-way down, the sun was reaching toward the top of the mountain opposite them. They rested on the rock shelf and watched darkness fill the valley and start up their mountain. Wind swept up the slope, cool and lively. It caught the saplings on both sides of them. Branches swayed, trunks leaned to one side and then the other, and leaves twirled in the slanting rays from the sun.

"When are Sheila and Timmy coming back?" Charlie said.

Boyd lay back, closed his eyes, and pointed his face into the sunshine. "They might stay in Philadelphia a while."

Boyd turned his head without raising it and looked at Charlie. "Guess you might as well know it all. She's left me, Dad." The morning hurt returned to Charlie's chest. Boyd turned his face back to the sun and closed his eyes. "Said she and Timmy will come back when we have a place to live. We're being evicted." Boyd laughed. "Can't even live in the car. It's been repossessed. After the first, I'm on the street."

Charlie closed his eyes and turned his face away.

"Fact is her folks can't pay," Boyd said. "Sheila's on Medicaid."

Charlie flinched.

"So I wanted to ask. . ." Boyd sat up. "Could you lend me a three or four thousand? I'll pay it back when things pick up." Boyd wore his crooked smile, but his eyes weren't smiling.

The wind whispered in Charlie's ears. He tried to hear its pitches. Instead, he saw Boyd hunkered on a curb, reaching out his hand.

"Steve knows?" Charlie said.

Boyd studied his boots.

The sun touched the top of the mountain to the west. The valley was black. The shadow reached toward them. The wind died, and calm settled over the land like a cool hand.

"It's getting dark," Boyd said.

When Charlie got to his feet, he realized how tired he was.

"What about the money, Dad?"

"Give me a while to let this sink in." Charlie shook his head. "You don't know, do you?" He studied the motionless black. "That's why your mother left me."

They stumbled down the trail into the shadow. Charlie glanced at the sky. The blue was turning to the mottled color of ripe peaches. He could hear Boyd's breathing behind him.

Twilight still hung in the air when they reached the camp. Boyd emptied the backpack of their lunch trash. Charlie sat at the camp table and listened to the creek.

"Boyd," Charlie said. "Bring us each a beer and sit for minute."

Boyd opened the cooler and took out two beers. He sat and handed one to Charlie.

"Boyd," Charlie said, "I'm not going to give you the money this time."

The smile on Boyd's face didn't change.

"It's time for you—" Charlie began.

Boyd turned toward the creek. The smile disappeared. He sat back, took a swallow of beer, and stretched. His eyes swept the sky. "Gets so quiet after dark. So quiet."

Charlie sighed and stood. "I'm going to see about dinner."

"Dad," Boyd said. Charlie stopped. Boyd put his elbows on the table and folded his hands. "What you say we break camp? We could be back before ten."

Charlie watched him. "You sure?"

Boyd nodded.

They drove without speaking. Boyd strummed and plucked. As they approached the city limits, he turned to Charlie. "You're a great dad. Always have been. I hope my problems won't change anything." He turned his gaze to the darkened horizon. "In my dream, when I was up on the stage and the crowd was going wild, I always looked through the faces for yours. I knew you'd be smiling and nodding." Boyd's voice wobbled. "I always wanted, more than anything in the world, for you to be proud of me."

Charlie wanted to cry. He looked at the stars hanging over the city ahead of them. He watched the orange arc lights whipping past with a slow rhythm all their own. He smelled the highway and the cars and Boyd and his own sweat. He listened to the tires singing on the pavement, a wavering A-flat.

Christmas in Hong Kong

Ferdie rolled on his side and licked his lips. Esther kept her body up. He'd give her that. As she slept next to him in the morning sunshine mottled by the willow outside the window, she was too beautiful for him to be pissed any more. She lay on her stomach in her peach silk nightgown, her face, turned toward him, serene. Her waist and butt were trim, her shoulders firm, her legs as shapely as when they'd met. He stretched close to her and put his arm across her shoulders. Her skin was warm and smooth.

Her eyes snapped open. "What are you doing?"

He pulled his hand back.

She sat up and pushed her hair out of her eyes. "Ferdie, you're too old for that."

No longer serene, she found her housecoat. "I'll get coffee going." She got as far as the door, then turned. "The Galloways have been complaining about King—you know, the Hansen's dog? They say he bit their child and nipped some kid down the street. I think we should just stay out of it. And maybe I could get you to move the flower pots from the cellar steps. I want to get the leaves cleaned out today."

"I'll clean them."

She was gone.

Ferdie flopped onto his back. The bed shuddered from his girth. An echo of last night's anger flitted through his belly. The greenhouse was his private preserve, the way some men had a den. Tina Hansen had no business futzing around in there and, worst of all, taking blooms from his rose standards. "She's more family than a neighbor, Ferdie," Esther had said. "Honestly, you're getting to be such a curmudgeon. Tina has the run of the house, like a relative. Like your daughter."

Not even my daughter has the run of the greenhouse. Mattie asks before she goes in there. Like she rings the doorbell instead of just flouncing in, and cleans up after she and Mikey have a snack.

Sometimes he felt like he was in a last ditch fight to hang on to what was left of *Ferdie*, the *man*, for Christ's sake. Yeah, it was Esther's house. Yes, she earned more than him, especially since they'd made him retire. And, yes, Tina was her best friend. But he'd never have allowed a child of his to behave the way she did. That electric-shock hair the color of cheap mahogany, those three-inch heels that arched her back and pushed her butt out, and the uplift bra that made her look like she needed a good exhale. But, goddammit, if that was what Esther wanted, he'd meet her half way.

He swung his feet to the floor and wobbled to the bathroom for his white terry cloth robe. Damn. He'd gotten a belly on him. That'd have to go. He was already twice Esther's size at normal weight. Made love making complicated. He stopped himself. She thought he was too old. Then why did he still want to?

Esther spent the morning going about her Saturday chores—sorting through unread mail, getting her clothes ready for the next week, confirming her afternoon appointments at the gym, and doing the endless "desk work" she'd brought home in her oversized briefcase—all the while listening to "good music." To Ferdie it sounded either prissy or ugly. Just when it'd get going on a good tune, it'd get all sour and scary sounding. Besides, what was all this "desk work?" Before he retired, he'd left his work at the nursery on weekends so Esther and he could relax together. Grumbling, he got the pot roast in the marinade, cleaned the leaves out of the cellar steps, and vacuumed the runner between the wall and stairway in the front hall. He'd have the afternoon to himself, to mow the lawn and work in the greenhouse, if he got the routine stuff done before lunch. But he couldn't wait to check on the fuchsias. "I'm going to run out to the greenhouse for a minute," he called to her at the foot of the stairs. No answer.

Out the kitchen door, down the steps, across the patio. The flagstones were still lodged in the dirt after three years. He'd done a good job. He stopped six feet from the greenhouse door. It was a thing of beauty, a miniature palace of moonstone and crystal all but invisible behind the yews and hollies. It housed life, growth, newness. He hurried in, closed the door behind him, and felt the warm, moist air settle on his skin. Hanging from pipes, his white fuchsia collection swayed gently in the diffused light. The two most mature specimens, now starting into bloom, were his joy. Mattie especially loved them . . .

Mattie. He had to call and confirm that she and Mikey were coming for dinner. He turned to the wall phone. They'd come. Mikey loved grandpa's marinated pot roast and apple cookies. Ferdie lifted the receiver.

Instead of a dial tone he heard Esther's voice. "God, I look forward to the time when he'll be gone."

Ferdie started to hang up. What? He put the receiver to his ear.

"I know what you mean," Tina's voice said. "All that huffing and puffing. God created the male ego on a bad hair day."

"No more manure stink," Esther said, "no more boots all over the closet floor, no more tent-sized terry cloth bathrobes on the bathroom door, no more sweaty sheets. And *flowers*. God, I'm sick of flowers. Why couldn't he have done something more, well, *manly*?"

"When's he going?"

"They reserved a spot in the campground for the Labor Day weekend. He'll be gone four days. Said he wanted Mikey to get to know the out-of-doors. I'll just chill out."

Tina laughed. "Why do men work so hard to make themselves disagreeable? When Stan's away, I celebrate."

"You know, Tina, sometimes—God forgive me—sometimes I look forward to being a widow, just being able to live the way *I* want . . ."

Ferdie replaced the receiver as quietly as he could. He lowered himself into the cast iron chair by the potting bench. Looking forward to being a widow?

When they'd married, he'd been a big Swede, all muscle and wavy blond hair with an oversized smile. Now the muscle had turned to droop, the hair was gray, and he'd forgotten how to smile. He was disappointed, too. When he divorced Mattie's mother, he'd promised himself he'd never marry again. Then Esther happened. He'd considered carefully, thought soberly and calmly. It looked right, so right.

He gave his head a fast shake, got to his feet, and fumbled with the hanging baskets. Numb, he found the new growth and pinched it back.

"Take the rocker," Ferdie said to Mattie. "Mikey always wants to be rocked."

Esther adjusted the elastic waist band on her grey sweat pants. "You three relax and enjoy yourselves. I've got a pile of desk work. Ferdie, leave the dishes. I'll get them in the morning."

"I'll get them after Mattie and Mikey head out. What did you think of the pot roast, by the way? I tried a little more garlic in the marinade."

"Nice meal, Ferdie. Thanks for all the work."

The soft pad of Esther's running shoes faded.

"It was better than nice, Dad," Mattie said from the rocker. She pushed her long chocolate-colored hair off her forehead. With her dark, shining eyes and that smile that always looked like it had a sob behind it and a voice always on the verge of breaking, she caught Ferdie's heart the way her mother had. "You've gotten to be a real cook," she said.

"Thanks, love. I'll introduce Mikey to tramp dinners while we're camping. You remember them?"

Her laughter sounded like water falling from stone to stone. "The only thing good about them is that they're cooked on a campfire."

"You love them and you know it. You think you should call Mikey in? It's getting dark."

She glanced at her watch. "I'll give him a few more minutes. Always so nice for him to come over here and spend time with you. He misses Jim. Sometimes he cries."

Ferdie winced.

"Jim'll have him at Christmas," she said. "That's the agreement. He's flying back from Munich to get him."

Ferdie sighed. "A world of single parents."

"Better than living in a world of sad marriages and sadder children. But you're one of the lucky ones. You and Esther have been together—what?"

"Twenty years this Christmas." He swallowed the raw spot in his throat. "What're you going to do at Christmas without Mikey?"

Mattie tilted back her head. Her hair fell away from her face. "I don't know. He's been my Christmas for the last six years. I've got plenty of time to think about it."

"You're welcome to stay with us. Or maybe you should go away. Paris or London or something."

"If I could afford it." She stopped rocking. "You know what I'd love to do? Go to Hong Kong for Christmas."

"Not exactly a christmasy place."

"That's what's so funky about it." She sat straight, closed her eyes, and hugged herself. "Christmas in Hong Kong. Doesn't that tweak your beak?"

He gave her a sidelong grin.

"Never mind," she said with a shrug. "Costs a bundle."

"Maybe you should settle for staying with us. Some-times—" His chest hurt. "Sometimes, we have to settle for less than we want."

Her mouth lost its smile. "What is it, Dad?"

"Nothing." He could feel a blush. "I just mean—" He shrugged.

"Is that what you're doing?"

He shrugged again. "Maybe. Sometimes we have to find good times where we don't even want to look."

"Creepy philosophy. Anyway—" She tucked her feet under the chair, grasped the arm rests, and rose. "Time to get Mikey in."

Ferdie followed her onto the porch. As he closed the door, he froze. Mikey's voice. Screaming.

Mattie dashed down the stairs.

Mikey was in the street stumbling backwards, his arms crossed before his face. A snarling russet dog, King from across the street, lunged and knocked Mikey backwards to the pavement. Mikey beat at the dog with his arms, but the dog, teeth bared, snapped at his face.

Ferdie was past Mattie and across the lawn in a blur. Still running, he brought his boot full force against King. The dog flew yelping in an arc and landed on the lawn of the Hansen's house and rolled. Mattie knelt beside Mikey. The dog started back. Ferdie headed toward him. The dog turned tail. Without breaking pace, Ferdie mounted the steps to the Hansen's porch and pounded. Fifteen seconds later, he pounded again. The door flew open and an angry Stan Hansen glowered out.

"Get rid of that dog," Ferdie bellowed, shaking with rage. "Hear me?"

Stan's face went white behind his full brown beard and horn-rimmed glasses. "What happened?"

"The goddamned dog just attacked my grandson. That dog goes, understand?"

"Now wait a minute, Ferdie—"

Ferdie spun and trotted back. Mikey was on his feet. Mattie was still on her knees beside him, one arm around him, stroking his hair with her trembling hand.

"He's all right," she said in a quaking voice. "Just shaken."

"Is he bitten?"

"Not deep enough to draw blood."

"Let's get him inside."

Panting, Ferdie scooped Mikey into his arms and turned his glare back to the Hansen's fake Victorian porch. Stan was still in the doorway as if stuck between the globe porch lights.

"You heard me, Stan," Ferdie yelled.

Stan slammed the door. Its Tiffany glass shuddered.

By the time they got to their own porch, Esther was in the doorway.

"He's okay," Ferdie said, pushing by her.

He carried Mikey toward the sofa. Mattie slipped past him, sat, and beckoned. Ferdie bent, ignoring the pain in his back, and set Mikey gently on Mattie's lap.

Ferdie straightened and allowed himself a sigh. Twinges ran through his back and legs. "How about some hot chocolate there, buddy?"

Mikey pressed his face into Mattie's breast.

"We got some cookies left," Ferdie said.

Mattie wagged one hand back and forth, palm out, in a not-now gesture.

Esther perched on the chair by the windows. "You think he should go to the emergency room?"

Mattie shook her head.

"Goddam dog—" Ferdie began.

"Ferdie. Your language," Esther said. "The boy—"

The doorbell startled them. Ferdie struggled to his feet and clomped to the door. Stan Hansen.

"Looks like the dog might have broken ribs," Stan said. "What did you do to him?"

Ferdie leaned his face closer to Stan's. "Kicked him away before he could rip out Mikey's throat. Why?"

Stan stood his ground. "Tina's taking him to the vet. I'm holding you responsible."

Ferdie placed one hand on Stan's shoulder and moved him backwards onto the porch. "Now, Stan, listen to me. I'm not going to tell you twice. Kill that dog. If I find him alive, I'll kill him. With my bare hands if I have to."

"I could sue. If King is seriously hurt—"

"You heard me."

Ferdie turned, went in, and closed the door quietly behind him.

Ferdie stood with his hand on the switch to the kitchen overhead light. One last look. His reward for hard work. The dish washer was humming away. The ebony cook top and Corian sparkled. The floor was freshly mopped. A tinge of Lysol spiced the air. Satisfied, he flipped off the light and headed into the living room. Esther was squatting by the sofa, rag and cleaning solvent in hand.

"Dishes done," he said. "Thought you were still working."

"Mikey soiled the sofa," she said.

"I'll get it."

"Done." She stood. "Ferdie, I want to talk to you."

"I wanted to check the hibiscus seedlings—"

"It's important."

With a sigh, he lowered himself into the recliner.

"I think you owe the Hansens an apology," Esther said.

"*I* think you got that backwards."

"They've been good neighbors. He's a respected lawyer, and her work for the Fielding Foundation is well known."

"You're serious."

"I've been working with Tina planning our anniversary party at Christmas. I was going to surprise you—"

Ferdie groaned. "Jesus, not a big fancy bash—"

"About ten couples. It's our twentieth."

He slid his bulk back in the recliner and tried to control his breathing. "I was hoping you'd be, well, you know, *proud* of me. I stood up to Stan. I kind of rescued Mikey. It was sort of, you know, *manly*. Not like flowers and all."

She nodded without looking at him. "I talked to Tina on the phone. King is territorial. He only goes after people he doesn't know. She suggested that Mattie and Mikey go over and let King get to know them—"

"So every stranger who comes to visit has to stop over and get chummy with King before—"

"Ferdie, be reasonable. She's trying to be helpful."

"Right."

Esther gritted her teeth. "She offered to get King in before we have visitors if we'll call and let her know—"

"Is everybody in the neighborhood going to clear visitors with the Hansens? Esther, we're not the problem. King's the problem. And King's the Hansen's problem. A biting dog has to go."

She stood, exasperated. "I might have known you'd take a crazy position like that. After the scene you made. And swearing in front of the neighbors."

He studied her. His stomach was cold. "I embarrassed you."

"Everything will be fine when we get things straightened out with the Hansens. Anyway, it's past bedtime."

"I'm going to check the seedlings," he said without moving.

"Can't it wait until morning?"

"I'm going to check the seedlings."

Inside the greenhouse, he closed the door and locked it behind him, then reached for the light switch but, on second thought, didn't turn it on. Instead, he sank into the cast iron chair. Light from the bulb on the back porch cast blurred images of limbs and branches and leaves on the frosted glass and filled the house with shadowless twilight. He couldn't see the Hansen's house from here. It was across the street, on the far side of his own house. Correction. Esther's house. Stan and Tina would be in bed by now. Would they be making love? Was Stan as much of a wimp as Ferdie? Were the Hansens happy? Was anybody ever happy?

He lifted a seedling in its peat pot from the perforated plastic tray and pressed the earth around the tiny stem with the tip of his finger. Too dry. Maybe he and Stan should run away together and leave Esther and Tina to the happy male-free existence they craved. Ferdie smiled without meaning to. He and Stan would escape to the south seas. Become beach bums. Have harems of nubile young dancing girls. Naw. Stan was too uptight. Even though Stan was fighting to hang onto what was left of his manhood, he didn't know it. Only in his forties. Too young to understand. But he wouldn't give in any more than Ferdie. He'd fight to the death to protect that fucking dog.

With practiced gentleness, Ferdie squeezed each peat pot. All too dry. He'd always thought that by the time people like him got into their sixties, they'd have solved their life problems and could settle down to mellow. In a few years he'd be seventy, and everything was coming apart.

At the back of the green house, he trickled water into the rubber bulb and returned to the chair. With all the tenderness he could muster into his big hands, his sprayed a mist onto the soil of the first seedling. He moved to the second. And Esther wanted to be a widow. He'd be damned if he'd accommodate her.

Two by two, he delicately grasped the peat pots and rear-ranged them, sprayed the bottom of their tray with a light fog of moisture, and lifted the tray to its shelf. Time to abandon his citadel and go to bed. Better wash his hands. Didn't want Esther to complain. As he heaved to his feet and moved to the sink, his back raised its perennial howl. He'd lie next to Esther, wanting her, knowing he couldn't touch her.

So this is what it was to be old.

On the way out, he hesitated. The telephone by the door was hardly visible in the half light. On impulse, he closed the door and locked it, lifted the receiver, and dialed Mattie's number by feel. When she answered, sleep hung in her speech.

"Sorry to wake you, honey," Ferdie said.

"Dad? Are you all right?"

"Been thinking. About Hong Kong. You really want to go?"

"Sure. But I told you—"

He nodded. "Thought so. This Christmas?"

"I can't afford it."

"I can."

"No, that's too much. I couldn't accept."

"What if the two of us went?"

Silence, then, "And Esther?"

"Just you and me, Mattie."

She was quiet. Then, haltingly, she said, "I thought you never wanted to be away at Christmas. Your anniversary and all."

He laughed. "Oh, that. What do you say? We could stay through New Year's."

"How're you going to afford it?"

"I'll borrow. How about it?"

"You're insane. And I'm crazy about you."

He hung up. Settled in the chair surrounded by soft light, he sat back and crossed his legs, daring his sacroiliac to give him trouble. He'd have to find a gym. Lots of hills in Hong Kong. He grinned. And maybe dancing girls. Sometimes, like he'd told Mattie, you have to find good times where you don't even want to look. Now all he had to do was figure out how to kill the fucking dog.

Snow and Ashes

The gray stone mansion rose from the trees like a palace that had snuck down the hill on a lark. I parked, per instructions from the landlord on the phone, in the slanting circular cobblestoned driveway. The house was silent, as if too proud to take notice of the riotous weeds at its foundation and the unkempt arborvitae all but blocking the windows. In the tunnel between the stoop and the front door, I found the bell embedded in a six-inch stone rosette.

One of the two doors swung open. Framed in the half-arch was a slim, bearded man in a tee-shirt over torn sweat pants. Shorter than me, he had shoulder-length sandy hair parted in the middle and pushed behind his ears, one of which sported an earring.

"Matt Stimson," I said. "I called about sharing the house."

The man gazed at me with a half-smile as though he recognized an old friend. "I'm Dan Spicer, the bourgeois landlord."

I followed him into a baroque foyer complete with a marble floor, a majestic staircase, and a dusty chandelier.

"Living room's to the left, study to the right. Both unfurnished." He headed toward a door set into the rear wall. "This is the dining room. It opens onto the veranda overlooking Creekside Park. Steps take you to the deck on the lower level.

From there you can walk down to the creek." As he stepped through the doorway, he tripped on the threshold and nearly fell.

I caught him by the elbow. "You all right?"

He laughed. "Haven't been all right for thirty-plus years. Why should I start now?"

We were in a long room lit by June sunshine flowing through French doors. Unmatched kitchen chairs surrounded three rough tables, none the same height, shoved together. An ancient television and boombox sat on milk crates at the end of the room.

"Grab a seat," Dan said, "and tell me about yourself."

I made it brief: ex-military, divorced, Masters in Special Ed, fourteenth year of teaching high school. Needed to be settled before the beginning of the school year in September. Hobby was weight lifting. Volunteer work with troubled children. Dan listened so intently that I wondered if he were hard of hearing.

"Only two of us living here now," he said, "not counting Michelle—she's only here weekends. Charlie—you'll have to meet Charlie. I'm the house Jew, and you'll be the gringo-*shaygets*-cracker. And Charlie . . . Charlie's just Charlie. We pretty much keep to ourselves. No shared meals or anything—"

The sound of scratching came from the French doors. Dan opened them and admitted a black German shepherd who reared and lapped his face.

"Down, Quasi." Dan struggled to maintain his balance. "This is the *man*. Name's Quasimodo."

The dog dropped to the floor with a thud. He cocked his head, sniffed, and padded toward me. When he placed his chin on my knee, I gingerly scratched the top of his head and behind his ears. He whined in pleasure.

Dan returned to his chair. "Freaky. Quasi's not all that friendly. In fact I've been training him to be a guard dog, you know, ready, attack—that kind of stuff."

I scratched harder. Quasi licked my fingers.

"Looks like you got his vote." Dan held out his hand, palm downward. Quasi lay on the floor.

"Your ad says sixteen-fifty a month," I said. "I can see why—it's a beautiful place—but I don't know that I can swing that much. You got a cheaper room?"

Dan's eyes were bright. "The small bedroom is eleven-fifty. Interested?"

"You bet. Can I see it?"

Before classes began, I was settled in a tiny bedroom on the second floor. The room at the end of the hall housed Charlie, and Dan's room was on the lowest level, beneath the dining room, opening to the deck, the back yard, and the park.

Charlie and I got acquainted one afternoon when we were both in the laundry room on the lower level. Turned out he had the mental capacity of a six-year-old and worked as a grocery store bagger. He'd moved his clothes to the dryer and couldn't get it to turn on. After he'd been fiddling with the controls for several minutes, I asked if he'd like me to see if I could figure them out. He watched me warily and finally nodded. The timer wasn't working—I had to push it hard to get it to turn. I showed him how to do it, and when he got the dryer started, he rewarded me with a beaming smile. From then on, Charlie always sat next to me at every opportunity. I got the feeling that he liked the idea that I was as big as he was.

Meanwhile, Dan treated me like a long-lost brother, and Quasimodo lavished me with more affection than I could handle. Michelle turned out to be a college junior at the university who was working as a lifeguard for the summer. She was majoring in European history and was delighted to learn that I had heard of the Esterházy dynasty. But I saw little of her—when her car was parked out front, neither she nor Dan was much in evidence.

On one of those bittersweet afternoons in late September when the leaves are telling you they know they have to die soon, I arrived home from school to find Dan lolling on the veranda off the dining room. Next to him was a mountain of blue ice and silver cans overflowing a galvanized tub.

"Hey, dude, ditch the tie and come tip a few," Dan called through the French doors. His speech was clipped and self-consciously precise, as though he were trying not to slur. "I bought a case. I'm cel-e-brat-ing."

"What's the occasion?"

"I'm a grad student and it's Tuesday."

I left my coat, tie, and briefcase in the dining room and crunched my way through scattered ice to the vacant chair beside him.

Dan snagged a can from the tub. Ice cubes flew like frightened birds. "Here you go, amigo." It slipped from his fingers, bounced once with a *thwack*, and rolled under his chair. He was on his hands and knees after it. "Goddammit." He clambered to his feet and grasped the ring on the can, trying to pop it open. I snatched it and ripped off the tab. Foam shot into the air and flowed over my hand. He wiped the can on his tank top.

"You're a grad student?" I asked.

Dan waved the question away. "Long story."

He finished his beer and reached for another, toyed with the tab, and gave me an apologetic smile. "Would you mind, bro?" He handed me the can.

I opened it. "How many have you had?"

"Stopped counting."

"Getting on toward dinner time. Maybe we should get some food into you."

"Not while there's brew waiting to be drunk," Dan said. "Chug-a-lug that and have another."

Charlie, dressed in overalls and work gloves, came through the door carrying pruning shears. When he saw me, he gave me his special smile.

"Doing the pruning?" I asked.

Charlie's smile turned proud. "I love doing it."

"Bet you do it like a pro," I said.

Still grinning, Charlie headed down the stairs into the garden.

When he'd disappeared, Dan turned to me, his eyes luminous. "You're, like, so good with Charlie."

I shrugged.

"He and I have an arrangement," Dan said. "He doesn't make much money so he does some chores around the house and I give him a break on his rent. He likes to take care of Quasi, but I don't let him do any of the attack training."

"How'd you meet him?"

Dan touched his beer can to his lips but didn't drink. "Let me tell you a story. My dad was a lion. By the nineteen-seventies when Sis—that's my older sister, Esther—and I were born, he'd built New Hope Drugs into a multi-million dollar business. But, me, I was a leftist rebel—dropped out, lived on the streets of San Francisco, and saw what happens to homeless disabled guys. Dad all but disowned me."

He wiped his mouth. "Then one day, Esther found me. She told me Dad had been diagnosed with amyotrophic lateral sclerosis, ALS—Lou Gehrig's disease. I went home, started classes again, majoring in Social Work. Dad was more and more disabled, but the old bastard refused to slow down. He died in a car accident. Sis and I suspect that he lost control and that's why it went into a telephone pole at forty miles an hour."

"Wow."

Dan stared into the trees. "He knew he was dying, so he set up everything for my mother and sister and me. When Mom died, Sis and her husband didn't want the house, so I took it. She and John got the furniture and most of the money except for a trust fund Dad had set up to keep me going until I finished school." He laughed. "Guess he never realized how long I'd drag out grad school working toward a PhD in social psychology and microeconomics. The main thing, though, was that I had this great house and for the first time in my life I could do something for guys who had no place to go. Then I found Charlie living on the street."

I winced. "So I'm one of your charity cases?"

Dan's face glowed the way it had during our first interview. "As soon as I saw you, when Quasimodo fell in love with you, I knew you were the right guy for this house, and—" He laughed. "I'm getting ahead of myself."

"Wait a minute," I said. "Why me?"

"Ask me when I'm sober."

"You drink like this when Michelle's around?"

"We've been having, like, difficulties," Dan said. "She might not be here this weekend."

"Maybe she doesn't like it when you drink."

Dan's eyes locked onto mine. "Just hang with me for a while, okay?"

He straggled to his feet and headed down the stairs toward his room, beer in hand. I watched him go. Alone, I finished my beer watching dusk settle over the back yard. Something wasn't right here, but I couldn't put my finger on it. With a shake of my head I squeezed my beer can until it collapsed and stood to gather the four cans Dan had left behind his chair. The weight of the first one told me it was still full. I checked the others. All full, with their tabs in place. Dan had opened them with a can opener.

Michelle did show up at the house on Friday evening. She and Dan cooked together and shared dinner on the deck. Saturday morning around eight, I went to the kitchen for coffee. Michelle was in the breakfast nook, newspaper in front of her. She wore jeans and a halter top showing off her deeply tanned skin, lambent in the morning light. Her amber hair was in a ponytail tied with a scarf.

"Look who's up and about," I said.

"Hi, Matt." She smiled. "Dan went back to sleep."

I took my coffee to the table. "Mornings are kind to you. You're positively glowing."

Her smile blossomed. "I'm in love."

"Not to overstep my bounds, but he's—what?—fifteen years older than you?"

"Who cares? Most women spend their whole lives without having what I have."

Charlie sidled in, his shy grin in place.

I heard the French doors in the dining room open, and Dan, frowsy with sleep, materialized in the kitchen doorway. "Was wondering where you disappeared to." He lumbered to the table and bent toward her. She smoothed his tousled hair.

He kissed her. "Let's take our coffee to the deck."

They left hand in hand.

Charlie watched them go and turned to me with tears in his eyes. "You help Dan, okay?"

"Help him—what?"

Charlie frowned at the floor and shambled out.

Sunday afternoon, I did laundry. When I transferred my clothes to the dryer, I couldn't get the timer to turn, no matter how hard I leaned on it. I made my way from the laundry room through the empty library to Dan's room. The sound of a television game show filtered through the door. I tapped. Quasimodo woofed, and the door opened.

"Hope I'm not interrupting," I said.

Dan waved me in. "Michelle headed home. We had a little . . . never mind."

The room was large, maybe twenty by twenty, with a door leading to the deck. An end table with a bong, a canister, and matches stood next to an unmade double bed.

Quasimodo advanced, tail wagging. I rubbed his head.

Dan beckoned. "Grab a chair."

I settled by the desk.

Dan flipped off the television and sat on the bed. His right leg jiggled.

I decided to make it brief. "The dryer's broken."

"I have a service contract. Number's on the laundry room wall. Call them."

"That was quick and easy. Thanks."

"I've been thinking," Dan said. "There's an apartment over the garage—used to be where the servants lived. It could really be nice if I could get it spruced up. You're out and about in the world. You know any down and out guys who need a place to live?"

"Why don't you and Michelle use it? It'd be a lot more—" The grimace on Dan's face stopped me. "None of my business."

"It's not that."

I waited.

"Anyway . . ." Dan shrugged. His fingers were trembling. I stood. "I'll call about the dryer."

As I turned to leave, I saw my reflection. An oversized mirror covered the door to the library.

With onset of autumn, my room, the smallest in the house, was getting crammed with books and student assignments. I asked Dan if I could move my workout bench and weights to the unfurnished living room—nobody ever went in there anyway—and did my regular workouts there three times a week.

Half way through my Monday night routine the first week in October, Dan, wrapped in his faded Army fatigue jacket, trudged in, beer in hand. He frowned while he waited for me to finish my military presses.

I dropped the dumbbells on the weight bench and paced between sets. "God, aren't you hot in that jacket?"

He walked with me but couldn't keep up. With a wrench of his shoulders, he lowered himself onto the bench and took a slug from the can. He couldn't sit still.

"You're acting like a teenager," I said, "with a bad case of the hornies."

"Need a favor, dawg. Guy's coming tomorrow at four to install the new dryer. Any chance you could be here to let him in? I've got a doctor's appointment."

I mopped my underarms, picked up the weights. "I'll come straight home from school. Get up. I need the bench."

He stood, leaned against the wall, and waggled his foot. I started my last set of presses. When I finished, I noted my weights, reps, and sets on my chart. Dan upturned his beer can into his mouth but the beer ran down his chin onto his neck.

He sat next to me on the bench and squeezed the can until his hand was shaking. It didn't crush.

"Will you sit still?" I slugged him lightly on the shoulder. "Looks like Michelle's holding out on you or something."

"We've been having, like, problems." He reached into the pocket of his jacket and pulled out another can.

I took it from him, pulled off the tab. "Man. I think you should lay off the booze." On my feet, I put the dumbbells in the rack, took two larger ones, and turned toward the bench.

Dan tossed the empty can across the room. "I might . . . Michelle and me might break up."

I stopped in mid-stride.

"She's a kid," he said. "Not ready for anything, like, serious, you know?"

"So who're you, Methuselah?"

Dan put his elbows on his knees and hung his head. "Feel like it sometimes."

"Be patient with her. She'll grow up." I draped my arm over his shoulder.

"Not fair, that's all. It's expecting too much."

"Dan," I said, "don't hurt her."

He lowered his face toward his spread knees and shuddered.

"What does *she* want?" I asked.

He shook his head.

I let go of him. I'd left a wet line across his shoulders. I took my towel from the bench and swabbed off the sweat.

He quivered like a dog shaking off water and got to his feet. "I'm going to get another brew, then see if I can get in some sack time."

"Had dinner?"

"Not hungry."

He started out. At the door, he stumbled, laughed, and straggled out of sight.

A November mild as May. Most evenings I spent as Rehearsal Manager for the school Winter Concert scheduled for mid-December, but on Veteran's Day, a holiday, Charlie and I shared the lower deck with the falling leaves for what we jokingly called "happy hour." As twilight faded, Charlie refused my offer of a Miller Lite: "Dan says I'm not supposed to drink that."

"We should ask Dan to join us," I said.

Charlie shook his head. "Michelle's here."

"What's up with them?"

Charlie blinked.

"Guess we should have held our party up on the veranda," I said. "Wouldn't want to disturb—"

"*No!*" A muffled yell. A woman crying out. Quasimodo barked. Dan's door flew open. Light stabbed the darkness. Figures in the doorway. Charlie whimpered. Dan and Michelle were shouting at each other, the dog barking and hopping.

I stood and called to them. "Hey, you guys, cut it out. Come on and have a brew with us."

"You don't like my religion," Dan yelled, "then fuck you."

"Why're you doing this?" Michelle cried.

"Bitch!" He swung back his arm as if to strike her. She ran to the stairs and sprinted to the veranda. Dan wobbled toward us. "Fuckin' bitch." He staggered through his door and slammed it.

Charlie was crying.

I dashed to Dan's door and pounded. "I want to talk to you." I tried the door. Open. On the threshold, I stepped on glass shards, kicked a full beer can. The mirror on the door to the library was a web of cracks reaching out from a five-inch hole in the middle. Dan was face down on the bed. His body was rigid, his face in the pillow next to his bloody fist. Quasi had his front paws on the bed, his ears thrust forward.

"Dan," I said.

"Go 'way, man."

"What the hell's going on?"

"The bitch won' leave."

I sat on the bed and put my hand on his shoulder. "She wants to be with you."

"Go 'way."

"Dan, you're plastered."

He flopped on his back. His face was twisted in rage, his teeth bared. "Get out."

"Let me—"

"*Quasi! Ready!*"

The dog sprang to the floor and turned toward me.

I edged from the room and closed the door. *What the hell*— I wandered into the darkness of the backyard toward the park. *Big trouble's brewing. If Dan keeps this up, he'll lose Michelle. But it isn't any of my business. The pieces don't fit together. It's almost as if Dan's drinking is the symptom of some other problem. Drugs? Something criminal?* I edged back onto the deck and bumped into someone. The sound of swallowed sobs stopped me. "Charlie?"

"Dan's my good friend," Charlie said in a choked voice.

"It's the booze," I said.

"Dan's sick. We gotta help him." Crying hard, he put his hand on my arm. "You help him, okay?"

For the rest of the week, I watched for a chance to talk to Dan while Charlie was tending to Quasi, but Dan stayed in his room and kept Quasi with him. No sign of Michelle. Charlie moped around the house like he was at a funeral. Sunday night, Michelle, minus her usual wave and smile, came in and went straight to Dan's room. I loitered on the deck but heard nothing. Finally, after dinner, I sat in the dining room with coffee trying to get caught up on grading papers. I was down to the next to the last essay when the sound of a slamming door made me look up.

Thumping and rattling. The French doors from the veranda flew open. Michelle weeping. Dan screaming at her. She careened into the room and ran headlong into the tables. Papers and coffee cup went flying. Dan, behind her, grabbed her hand and yanked her toward him. She shrieked. I leaped to my feet and blocked his arm as it swung to strike her.

"You out of your fuckin' mind?" I yelled.

"Get out, bitch," Dan rasped.

She wrenched her hand free and raced out the door to the foyer. Footsteps, then the front door banged.

Panting, I turned to Dan. "What the hell's the matter with you?"

Tears streaked his face. "I did it. She's gone. She won't be back."

With a tremor, as if from old age, he shuffled in place until he was facing the French doors. He staggered through them. Dragging footsteps across the veranda and then his uneven footfalls down the stairs. I heard him open the door to his room. He was sobbing.

The following night I had parent-teacher conferences, so I got home past nine. As I let myself in, Quasi's bark, unexpectedly close, made me jump. The dog, poised by the open door to the study, wagged across the foyer. I went to the study. In what had been a bare room were Dan's bed with him in it, his desk and computer, and his chair.

He raised his hand in greeting. "Welcome, brother."

"Don't 'brother' me. After last night—"

Sadness filled his face. "Matt . . . please?"

"Why'd you move up here? How—"

"Come on in and close the door. Charlie helped me. I've been waiting for you."

I shut the door and sat. Quasi put his paws on my knee and licked my face.

"Quasi," Dan said, "behave."

The dog immediately dropped to the floor but looked up at me. I petted him.

"I was sure that first day," Dan said, "that you were the man. Quasi picked you." He slid to a sitting position. "I pretty much knew by last spring what I had to do. Nobody I knew could take it on. You know what I'm saying?"

I scratched the top of my head. "Haven't the foggiest."

"Thought maybe you'd sorted it out. The drinking freaked out everybody except you."

"I couldn't believe you were a crunk head."

"Get comfortable. This'll take a while." At a flat-hand signal from Dan, Quasi lay on the floor and rested his chin between his paws. "First, I want your promise that nothing I tell you will leave this room. No one is to know. Not Charlie, nobody."

"Why?"

"I don't want any leaks that might get to Michelle. Let her think I'm the bastard who kicked her out. You promise?"

"I don't get it," I said.

"Say it."

"I promise."

He looked past me. "When Dad realized he was dying, he put both Sis and me on the New Hope Medical Plan in perpetuity. He knew that with his version of ALS there was a chance that the genetic disposition would be passed on. Sis's home free. I'm not."

I didn't move.

"You understand?" he asked. "I've got it. Lou Gehrig's Disease."

I opened my mouth. No sounds came.

"There are about ten tests," he said, "They subjected my beautiful male body to magnetic resonance imaging, put needles into my muscles, gave me electric shocks, scanned my brain, tapped my spine, x-rayed me until my piss sparkled. The symptoms are increasing faster than they expected. Until last month, they thought I'd have another year. Now they're not sure. They put me on Riluzole a year ago to slow the disease down. Didn't work."

"Your sister knows?"

He nodded. "When things get bad, I'll go to her place in Cleveland."

"Michelle—"

"No. She's not to know."

"Dan, that's not fair."

"She's only twenty, Matt. She doesn't need this. If I'd known . . ."

"What do you want me to do?"

"Let everybody think I'm drying out. I'll need your help. Like, I can't put my shoes on. I moved up here because I can't manage the stairs anymore. Check in before you leave for school and after you get in at night. Don't go around looking like the angel of death. Do your usual bullshit—you know, like, school stuff and weights and everything." He watched me without blinking. "Fair enough?"

I nodded. "Sooner or later it's going to be obvious—"

"That's when I clear out. I want you to take Quasi when I . . . go to Sis's. You and Quasi are made for each other."

"What about the house? Your stuff?"

He waved his hand. "Later. Any other questions?"

"When'd you find out?"

"I began noticing symptoms three years ago. Scared the hell out of me. For a long time, I didn't get tested. I didn't want to know. One night last winter, I fell down the stairs. Told Michelle I was drunk. That's when I went in for the full battery. They sent me to Johns Hopkins. One by one, all the other explanations were ruled out. About the time you moved in, I couldn't button my shirt. So I wear tees and tanks. That's when I decided Michelle had to go."

"Don't you think she'd want to know?"

"You don't understand. At the end, you can't sit up anymore. You can't talk. You can't take a shit without help. Your mind and your cock function just fine, thank you, but your breathing muscles shut down. You die of suffocation. They give you morphine so you won't panic as you're dying. You want me to put her through that?"

I fought off a shudder.

He tilted back his head. "I don't want her ever to know. When the time comes, tell her I'm in California. Taking courses at Stanford. Something I always wanted to do. She'll believe it. But. . . Matt . . ." He leaned forward. "Check on her, okay? Be sure she's all right?" He sighed. "That's enough for now. Be sure to say good night to Quasi. Leave the door open so he can get out. I'll need your help in the morning." His eyelids fluttered. "I want to wear jeans sometimes, but I can't zip my fly."

As the days grew short and the nights cold, Dan pretty much stopped leaving the study except to go to the bathroom. I told Charlie he had the flu, then hinted that it had turned into pneumonia. Charlie just looked at me, his face blank.

When I got in from school one icy December night, I tapped at the study door and went in. The room was dark. The air was sickly sweet with marijuana smoke.

"Leave the light off," Dan said, "and close the door."

As soon as I sat, I felt Quasi's head on my knee. I chafed behind the ears and heard the growl of bliss.

"Called Sis today," Dan said, "Told her I'd be flying out there on the nineteenth. That's a Wednesday. Can you drive me to the airport?"

"Sure."

"I won't be able to make it to the bathroom much longer. And there are some things I won't ask you to do."

"I'd be willing," I said.

"No. It's decision time, Matt. Only three things I care about. Michelle, that's done. Quasi, he'll be with you. The house. I know what I want to do."

Water gurgled. A spot glowed red on the table. The bong. "Here's the deal. This place has become a refuge for Charlie. I wanted to look for other guys like him. Then I found out I was sick, and I didn't know how I was going to keep it going. I knew somebody'd have to take it over. Then I found you." He sucked, held his breath, released the air from his lungs. "So I want to sell you the house."

I laughed. "I haven't got that kind of money."

"How does one dollar sound?"

Quasi nudged my hands with his nose. I'd stopped moving.

"Sis doesn't want the house," Dan said. "Dad's law firm will handle the details. You have to promise to keep the place as a refuge for Charlie and men like him."

"Why me?"

"You're the kind of man I always wanted to be. I watched you with Charlie. You kept my secret. I trust you." He paused and sucked. "And Quasi chose you."

Grassy fumes stung my eyes.

"Get the apartment fixed up," Dan said, "and move into it. Then when you hook up with a woman, you'll have a beautiful place to share with her. That's what I wanted to do with Michelle before I found out . . ." He swallowed. "No one is to know about this as long as I'm living. I'll tell Charlie I've asked you to fill in for me while I'm away. He doesn't need to know I'm not coming back."

"I think Charlie already knows."

Silence, then, "He would, wouldn't he? Poor guy. I love that pitiful son-of-a-bitch."

I arranged for a sub to take my classes on the nineteenth. I got up early, fixed Dan breakfast, got him into jeans and a sport shirt with buttons. After I helped him into his coat, I carried his luggage to the foyer.

"It's time," I said.

"No hurry," Dan slurred. He licked his lips and said with careful enunciation, "Help me up."

With me at his side, he shambled to the foyer. "Except for my time on the street, I lived my whole life in this house. Take better care of it than I did, okay, Matt?" At the front door, he grasped my hand. "Do something for me. When Quasi dies, have him cremated and spread his ashes on the back lawn."

I helped him into the passenger seat, locked his seat belt, and headed out. While we were on the freeway, I glanced at him. His hands were tightly clasped and he was gazing straight ahead. As we slowed for the airport exit, he turned to me.

"You've been great. Wish you could come with me."

"Other folks can do more than I can."

"I only want to say, like, you know, thanks. Especially for agreeing to take the house and look after Charlie."

The airport sign blurred past. I pulled up in front of the terminal. A uniformed airline agent waited with a wheelchair. I put the car in neutral, hopped out, and helped Dan into the chair.

"This is it, buddy," Dan said.

"I'll park and come in."

"No way. Does it embarrass you to be hugged by a man in public?"

I knelt on the sidewalk.

Dan clutched me with shaking arms and held me tight. "So great you came along when you did, Matt. So great."

I wanted to thank him for everything but couldn't find my voice. The attendant wheeled the chair toward the glass doors. As they went through, Dan swiveled, saluted, and smiled casually, as though he were leaving for the weekend.

All the way home, I had to blink to clear my eyes. How long would it be? I hoped they'd give Dan enough morphine that he'd sail away from life high, tripped out, zonked like endless orgasm.

Without Dan the house felt like a soulless shell. Charlie and I gave Christmas a token celebration and ignored New Years.

By mid-January, I'd run out of things for Charlie to do, so he and I started refurbishing the apartment. He was a hard worker and stronger than me. Looked to me like we could have the place shaped up by summer. When we got the larger of the two bedrooms painted, I took pictures and emailed them to Esther. February brought heavy snows, so I worked alone in the apartment and had Charlie keep the driveway, the steps, and the walks shoveled.

Late one Wednesday afternoon, the phone rang.

"Matt? This is Esther, Dan's sister." Her voice wavered. "I knew he'd want me to tell you right away. He's dead."

My throat closed.

"This afternoon he took the car keys from my purse," Esther said. "I don't know how he got the car out of the garage, much less on the road. Went into a telephone pole about a mile from here. Killed instantly."

"Esther—"

"His speech was failing. Next week he was going to have a feeding tube implanted and be fitted for a mask to help him breathe."

Maybe she needed to talk. It hurt to listen.

"He was so grateful to you," she said. "He loved the pictures of the apartment. Last night he asked me . . ."

Her voice failed. I waited.

"He asked," she went on, "that you and I spread his ashes on the back lawn—if you agreed."

"Of course."

"John and I could fly down a week from Saturday and do it Sunday."

I hesitated. "Esther, did Dan say anything? Before he took the car?"

"No, but he wouldn't have. No notes or anything."

"So we'll never know—"

"We know," she said.

It took me a long time to pull myself together. When I could talk without crying, I went looking for Charlie. I found him in the kitchen eating cereal.

"The phone call was Esther, Dan's sister. He's dead, Charlie. Killed in a car accident."

Charlie wept soundlessly.

On the appointed Saturday, I met John and Esther at the airport and settled them in Dan's old room. We agreed that Dan would want the scattering to be done without ceremony. The following morning, we gathered in the dining room. Esther, in jeans and a parka, sat next to John, a polished wooden case twice the size of a cigar box in her lap. Charlie, somber but dry-eyed, said nothing.

"It was a pleasure to meet you, Charlie," Esther said.

"Charlie is Dan's kind of people," I said.

Esther smiled. "I know."

The four of us passed through the French doors to the veranda, freshly cleared of snow by Charlie, and moved down the stairs, then fanned out in a semi-circle on the snow-covered lawn. Quasi stood beside me. The sky darkened and fresh snow flurried down on us.

"Dan didn't want any prayers or eulogies," Esther said. "He wanted Matt and me to share the spreading of his ashes—"

She looked at the house. Quasi, suddenly alert, woofed.

Coming down the stairs from the veranda was a woman in a black turtleneck and jeans. Her honey-colored hair was pulled into a ponytail. Quasi streaked across the yard, spinning snowflakes in his wake, and bounced up the steps. Whimpering, he rose on two legs, plumped his paws on her shoulders, and lapped her face.

"Michelle," I said in a hoarse whisper. "How did—"

"I called her this morning," Esther said.

"Dan didn't want her to know."

"I did."

Michelle told Quasi to heel. They descended the steps together, and she hugged Charlie and me. "I got here as soon as I could."

"I'm sorry," I said. "Dan made me promise—"

She shook her head, put her arms around me, and rose on tiptoe to kiss me. Then she faced Esther. "Thanks, Sis. May I call you Sis?"

Esther's face cracked. She ran the back of her hand over her eyes and handed Michelle the box. "You scatter his ashes. Matt and I will help."

As Michelle opened the box, the snowfall thickened. The three of us started at one end of the lawn and walked side by side, casting handfuls of gritty ashes. Quasi, head down, stayed close to Michelle. When we reached the end, we reversed direction. Two-thirds of the way on the second pass, the box was empty. Charlie put his arm around Esther.

Michelle watched the flakes cover Dan's ashes. Then she turned toward the stairs to the veranda. We followed. I brought up the rear. Half way up, I glanced over my shoulder. Quasi stood on the deck looking at the lawn. He raised his head and sniffed the air, then trotted to me and licked my hand.

Publication History

"The Gift of the Father"

First published in *Seven Hills Review*, 2005. Finalist for the 2004 Greensboro Awards in Short Fiction. Second place in the 2005 *Wild Violets* competition. Third place in the 2004 Seven Hills Contest for Writers. Reprinted on the WriteCorner Press website with Tom Glenn as featured writer.

"Best Buddies"

The Lantern (Summer 1998). The story was reprinted in *Scribble* (April 2000).

"Trip Wires" *Antietam Review* (Spring, 1999) (*Antietam Review* nominated this story for the 1999 Baltimore ArtScape Literary Arts award.) Republished in Tom Glenn's novel-in-short stories, *Friendly Casualties* (Amazon.com, September, 2012).

"Fuchsias" *The Baltimore Review* Volume II, Number 2 (Summer 1998)

"Jolly, Jolly Sixpence" *Pangolin Papers* (Spring 2005) (This story was selected from among 19,000 for Honorable Mention in the 2002 Writer's Digest competition.) Republished in Tom Glenn's novel-in-short stories, *Friendly Casualties* (Amazon. com, September, 2012).

"E-Square" *BrickStreet* Vol 1, No. 1 (May, 2002)

"The Song of the Earth" *Potpourri* (Fall, 2003—website)

"Wolf Rock" *Fodderwing* (2001) Honorable mention, 2008 Washington Writing Prize; reprinted in *The Book of Scars: 2007 Prose Collection Book* as a Scars Publications Editor's Award Winner; first place in the Hackney Literary Awards national short story competition for 2000.

"Christmas in Hong Kong" *Potpourri* Vol 13, No. 4 [December, 2001]

"Snow and Ashes" published in 2016 by the *Loch Raven Review*. Finalist for the Alexander Patterson Cappon Prize for Fiction, August 2014. Third place in New Voices International Fiction Writing Contest 2014. Semifinalist in the 2010 Dana Awards.

About the Author

Dr. Tom Glenn has worked as an intelligence operative, a musician, a linguist (seven languages), a cryptologist, a government executive, a care-giver for the dying, a leadership coach, and, always, a writer. Much of his writing comes from the years he shuttled between the U.S. and Vietnam as an undercover NSA operative supporting army and Marine units in combat before escaping under fire when Saigon fell.

Between 1962 and 1975, Glenn was in Vietnam at least four months every year. He had two complete tour there and so many shorter trips that he lost count. He was a civilian employee of the National Security Agency, but his when in Vietnam, he was under cover as an army or Marine enlisted man; to maintain his cover, NSA redacted his name from its public documents. He was sent to Vietnam repeatedly because he knew North Vietnamese radio communications intimately—he'd been exploiting them since 1960. He spoke Vietnamese, Chinese, and French, the three languages of Vietnam, and he was willing to go into combat with the army and Marine units he was supporting all over South Vietnam. After the withdrawal of U.S. military forces from Vietnam in 1973, he headed the covert NSA operation there. As the fall of Saigon loomed in April 1975, he evacuated his 43 subordinates and their families even though the U.S. ambassador, Graham Martin, had forbidden him to send his people out. On the night of April 29, after all his people were safely out of the country and the North Vietnamese were already in the streets of the city, he fled by helicopter under fire.

What Glenn did after the end of the Vietnam war in 1975 is still classified. But it is public information that he toured the country lecturing on leadership and management, trained federal executives, and was the Dean of the Management Department at the National Cryptologic School. Maryland Public Television interviewed him and fifteen others in its 2016 salute to Vietnam vets, and his memoir article on the fall of Saigon has been published by *Studies in Intelligence* and reprinted in the *Atticus Review* and the *Cryptologic Quarterly*. In late 2017, the *New York Times* featured his story on his role in the 1967 battle of Dak To in Vietnam's central highlands. These days he is a reviewer for the *Washington Independent Review of Books* and the *Internet Review of Books* where he specializes in books on war and Vietnam. His Vietnam novel-in-stories, *Friendly*

Casualties, is now available on Amazon.com. Apprentice House of Baltimore brought out his novels *No-Accounts* in 2014 and *The Trion Syndrome* in 2015. In 2017, the Naval Institute Press published his novel, *Last of the Annamese*, set during the fall of Saigon. Adelaide Books brought out his latest novel, *Secretocracy*, in early 2020. You can access his blog at https://tomglenn.blog/

www.ingramcontent.com/pod-product-compliance
Lightning Source LLC
Chambersburg PA
CBHW020023030726
47499CB00007B/2252